# SERVANTS OF THE EMPIRE

## THE SECRET ACADEMY

BY JASON FRY

EGMONT

*We bring stories to life*

First published in Great Britain 2015
by Egmont UK Limited, The Yellow Building,
1 Nicholas Road, London W11 4AN.

Cover illustration by Jim Moore



ISBN 978 1 4052 7781 5
60270/1
Printed in UK

Find more great *Star Wars* books at www.egmont.co.uk/starwars

# PART 1:
# ZARE

# CHAPTER 1

**'*Hey,* kid – wake up.'**

For a moment Zare Leonis couldn't remember where he was. He should have been in the barracks in Lothal's Imperial Academy with his fellow cadets. But instead he was sitting by himself, strapped into a harness.

Then it all came back to him. He was in an Imperial shuttle. The man impatiently telling him to wake up was an Imperial pilot. And the shuttle had completed the short journey from Lothal to Arkanis, where Zare was due at the officers' academy.

'Right,' he said, still a bit foggy. 'Sorry.'

He unbuckled his harness and yanked his duffel bag out from under his seat. The broad door in the side of the shuttle opened with a whine of servos. It was pitch-black outside and rain lashed Zare's face.

The cold startled him and he peered into the darkness uncertainly.

'I've got a schedule to keep,' the pilot grumbled.

A bolt of lightning zigzagged across the sky, giving Zare a brief glimpse of the landing pad half a metre beneath the shuttle. He jumped down, bending his knees against the shock of the landing. The door behind him instantly closed, and the shuttle's engines began to rise in pitch.

Zare stepped aside, one arm over his face in a vain effort to ward off the rain. His white cadet's uniform was already soaked through. As the shuttle rose into the night, lightning split the sky and a crack of thunder made Zare jump. The flash left him with a brief impression of buildings surrounding a rectangular open area. He peered through the dark, shivering and wondering where he was supposed to go.

Lightning struck again and Zare jumped, crying out involuntarily. A droid with glossy black plating was standing still and silent on the landing pad, ignoring the storm around them.

'You scared me half to death,' Zare said. 'Why didn't you say something?'

He waited for the next flash of lightning to give him another look at the droid. When it came, he wished it hadn't – the droid didn't seem to have a face, just two black photoreceptors in a featureless expanse of metal.

'I am DDM-38,' the droid said in a vaguely female monotone. 'I will take you to your dormitory.'

And then, without another word, DDM-38 strode off into the howling rain. Zare hurried to keep up, his boots squelching in the muddy ground. Thunder rolled and lightning flickered. The buildings around them looked like stone.

'This place looks old,' Zare said. 'When was the Academy founded?'

'The Academy was established sixty-three years ago,' said DDM-38. 'But some of its buildings were part of a fortress established before Republic contact.'

'A fortress? Built by whom?'

'A native species,' DDM-38 said. 'They are extinct.'

'Oh,' Zare said. The lightning revealed buildings on three sides of them; in the other direction Zare saw a dark expanse of sea, broken by a stone tower rising out of the shallows, perhaps thirty metres offshore.

'What's over there?' he asked, pointing.

'The tower is forbidden to cadets.'

'Forbidden? Why?'

The droid said nothing, striding through the howling rain.

'DDM?' Zare said. 'I asked why the—'

'Stay off the beach. It is not safe. This is your assigned dormitory.'

Zare followed the black-plated droid up a short flight of stone steps into a building. He sighed, grateful to be out of the rain. DDM-38 reached up and the lights came on, revealing a long room filled with bunks. Groans and protests filled the air as teenage cadets flung up their arms, squinting at the new arrivals.

'Turn it off – I can find my way,' protested a crestfallen Zare, aware of the glowers aimed in his direction. But DDM-38 ignored him, striding across the barracks. Zare followed, leaving a trail of water in his wake.

'This is your bunk and locker,' DDM-38 said. 'Your standard field and dress uniforms have been prepared based on your measurements. Breakfast is at 0600.'

'But I just got here,' Zare said, looking at the droid in disbelief. It was late afternoon on Lothal but just after 0400 on Arkanis.

'Officers deal with far worse hardships,' DDM-38 said, then turned and strode back the way she'd come, metal feet ringing on the stone floor, ignoring the cadets' muttering. She shut the door behind her, leaving the lights on.

Cheeks hot, Zare hurried across the dormitory and shut off the lights, then picked his way back to his bunk. He unzipped his duffel and hunted for a towel, trying not to drip on his bed, then shuffled across the room to the dimly lit bathroom.

He wondered how many of his fellow cadets he'd already alienated, then snorted at himself as he ran the towel over his dark, wiry hair.

*You're not here to make friends,* he reminded himself. *You're here to find Dhara and bring her home.*

Zare's sister, Dhara, was a year older than he was and had enrolled at Lothal's Imperial Academy while Zare was at the Junior Academy for Applied Sciences, waiting for his own chance to serve the Empire. Dhara had been a top student at the Imperial Academy – and then she'd disappeared.

The Empire said she'd run away during a training exercise, but by the time Zare had arrived at the Academy he'd known the story was a lie – just like he'd known the Empire had lied about many other things. With the help of his girlfriend, Merei Spanjaf, Zare had discovered that Dhara was kidnapped as part of something called Project Harvester and taken to Arkanis by the ruthless Imperial agent known as the Inquisitor. All because she was sensitive to the Force – something none of the Leonises had ever suspected.

Zare had done well enough at Lothal's Academy to earn a midyear transfer to Arkanis. But he'd taken a dangerous gamble to do so – he'd made the Inquisitor think he was Force-sensitive, too. It terrified Zare to think what would happen if the Inquisitor discovered that wasn't true.

Zare stripped off his soaked uniform and scrubbed himself with the towel, trying to keep his teeth from chattering. Was Dhara somewhere nearby, there at the Academy? He didn't know – and he doubted even Merei would have been able to find out. She'd discovered what had happened to Dhara by slicing into the Empire's databases, but there were limits to what even a talented slicer such as Merei could discover about the Empire's most secret projects.

And besides, he and Merei had broken up before he left Lothal. That was Zare's fault – he'd become so obsessed with finding his sister that he'd stopped considering the perils Merei faced and how much they frightened her. When she'd needed him most, he'd barely noticed.

*And now it's too late – too late for me and Merei and maybe too late for Dhara. I don't even know if she's still alive.*

Zare stared into the mirror for a moment, registering the bags under his eyes. He was so tired – he could feel exhaustion like an ache in his bones. Tired and scared – scared that he'd made nothing but mistakes. He'd been a fool to lose Merei and an even bigger fool to go to Arkanis. Sooner or later he'd be caught and his deception revealed.

He should just give up. He'd tried as hard as he could – no one could ask more of him than he'd given. It was hopeless. It always had been.

*No. No it isn't.*

He turned away from the mirror, disgusted with himself. He would find Dhara – no matter how tired he was or how long the odds were. Now that he was there, all he could do was keep going.

*Too bad I have no idea what to do next.*

Footsteps sounded behind him as he was pulling a T-shirt over his damp hair. A handsome young cadet nodded at him sleepily. Zare guessed he was a couple of years older than his own sixteen years.

'So you're the new transfer,' the boy said, extending his hand. 'Orman le Hivre.'

'Zare Leonis. Sorry I woke everybody up.'

'That was DeeDee's fault, not yours,' le Hivre said with a smirk, his pale blue eyes studying Zare. 'You shouldn't even bother drying off, you know – you'll be wet the whole time you're on this miserable planet.'

'You mean it rains like this all the time?' Zare asked.

'Like this? No – this only happens two or three times a week. Usually it's just drizzling. Unless there's fog. Or sleet.'

'Terrific.'

Le Hivre smirked again. 'You better get some sleep, Leonis. We've got live-fire exercises in the afternoon. It wouldn't do to take a blaster bolt to the head because you're yawning.'

# CHAPTER 2

**Breakfast came** far too soon, and a groggy Zare got a bowl with porridge in the mess hall and looked around at the tables filled with cadets. There were more than seventy cadets in all, wearing grey uniforms with white stripes above carefully polished boots.

He spotted le Hivre sitting at a table that was only half-full, but the moment he put his tray down there, the mess hall went silent. Everyone was staring at him.

'You can't sit here,' said a wiry-looking boy to le Hivre's right. 'You're not one of us.'

'What does that mean?' Zare asked, embarrassed and baffled – and a little angry.

'Leonis is new, Rav,' le Hivre said, then smiled at Zare. 'But it's true that you can't sit here. You'll understand soon enough.'

'If you're good enough,' Rav said, turning back to the other cadets at the table as if Zare weren't there.

Zare picked up his tray, his cheeks hot. He walked through the mess, feeling the other cadets' eyes on him.

'Hey, new guy,' said a boy about Zare's age with red hair and a startling number of freckles. 'You can sit with us.'

The boy's tablemates shifted and Zare sat down gratefully, nodding at the new cadets. The red-haired boy was Penn Zarang. His tablemates introduced themselves as Tigard Manes, Bedal Cerroux, Chan Harra, and Anya Razar. Zare dug into his porridge, wishing he'd put more sweetener in it, and let the conversation buzz around him.

'Where did you transfer from again, Leonis?' Penn asked. 'Andooweel?'

'Lothal,' Zare said.

'Never heard of it.'

'I hadn't, either, until we moved there,' Zare said. 'Where are you from?'

He'd never heard of two of their homeworlds, but the squat, sad-eyed Bedal Cerroux was from Eriadu, an important trade world in the Outer Rim. And gangly, ash-blonde Anya Razar was from Coruscant.

'So this is a little different than home,' Zare said.

Anya shrugged. 'It's only for the rest of the year. After that I'll be a junior cadet on Raithal.'

'So you keep telling us,' said Tigard, folding his muscular arms over his chest. 'What happens if you're wrong?'

'I won't be,' Anya said. 'Just watch. I won't be at this table much longer, for starters.'

Her eyes jumped to where le Hivre sat.

'What's so special about that table anyway?' Zare asked, and the five cadets looked at him.

'It's the commandant's table,' Penn said quietly. 'It's reserved for the Commandant's Cadets.'

'And how do you get to be a Commandant's Cadet?'

Nobody said anything. Zare looked from one cadet to another.

'You get invited,' the tall, pale Chan finally said, and from the cadets' expressions Zare knew none of them had been.

'Invited and tested,' Bedal said.

'Tested how?' Zare asked.

Penn started to answer, but Anya cut him off.

'It's not something we talk about here,' she said, then smiled. 'Anyway, Penn here doesn't know and never will. They don't invite people who can't stay off academic warning.'

Penn stared down at his tray morosely. Around them, cadets started getting up in twos and threes.

'Wake up, Cadet Leonis,' Anya said with a smile that Zare could have interpreted as friendly or mocking. 'Time for class.'

It wasn't raining, but a thick fog cloaked the academy buildings. Zare checked his datapad and saw he had Strategy and Tactics with Colonel Julyan. He asked around until he found cadets who had the same class, then followed them across the sodden lawn of pale green moss to a stone building on the other side of the grounds.

Julyan was cadaverous and bald, with a drooping white moustache. He sat behind a hovering lectern, his lower body wrapped in a black blanket.

'Settle down, cadets,' he barked, raising the lectern higher into the air so he was looking down at the rows of boys and girls. 'When last we left Admiral Screed, the navy had driven the Iska pirates from Fanha and smashed them at Tosste. Now, let's discuss the Battle of Ogoth Tiir. It's node thirty-three in your datapads.'

Julyan was a restless lecturer, swooping around the room as he talked, summoning up holographic representations of contested sectors and battlefields and calling out cadets' names in turn to question them about decisions made by Imperial commanders. Did they agree with the strategy? No? Then what would they have done differently?

It was more intense than anything Zare had experienced on Lothal, and despite his exhaustion he found himself responding to Julyan's rapid-fire narration, trying to anticipate his questions and watching his fellow cadets. They kept their eyes focused on Julyan, tapping at their datapads and thrusting their hands in the air to argue various points with him. Zare found it fascinating – and thrilling.

*Remember why you're here,* he thought. *It's not to learn how the pacification of Bryndar could have gone differently.*

'Cadet Horan, that's the second time you've mentioned leadership today,' Julyan said to the wiry boy from the commandant's table, the one le Hivre had called Rav. 'That's a quality we'd all agree is important, yet have trouble defining. Cadet Leonis, I have a question for you.'

'Yes, sir?' Zare asked, startled. A moment later Julyan was hovering in front of Zare, peering down at him with dark eyes.

'You were centre striker on a grav-ball team that won a league championship, Cadet Leonis,' Julyan said. 'Isn't that right?'

Zare nodded sombrely. He'd won that title with AppSci a little over a year before, with Merei and Beck Ollet as his teammates, but it felt like a lifetime had passed since then.

'And what did you learn as centre striker that will make you a better Imperial officer?'

Zare considered that for a moment.

'To improvise, sir,' he said. 'There's no game plan that survives contact with the other team. You have to see what works and what doesn't. You adapt – and then you keep adapting.'

'As every team must,' Julyan said. 'And why do some succeed while others fail? Come on, Cadet Leonis. A lot of people would say it's a simple question.'

'With respect, sir, I don't think it is.'

Julyan offered him a wolfish grin.

'I don't think it is, either, cadet. But answer it anyway.'

'Well, sometimes it's luck, sir,' Zare said. 'We don't like to think so, but it's true. But that aside, the most important thing is the quality of the players – followed by the leadership shown. As centre striker I had to trust that my players would execute their parts of the plan – but they had to trust me that the plan was sound.'

'So you're a leader, then? Come now, Leonis – don't

give me that look. Modesty in an officer candidate is useless.'

'I have been a leader, sir,' Zare said. 'But this isn't about me. I suspect everyone in this room has proved himself or herself a leader – if they hadn't, they wouldn't be here. The important thing is figuring out who's the right leader to execute the plan, and for everyone to accept that and do their duty.'

'Well said, cadet,' Julyan said. 'Which brings us to the leadership shown by General Romodi in the aftermath of Ogoth Tiir. Turn to node thirty-six and let's discuss his reconstruction initiatives.'

As the cadets tapped at their datapads, Zare saw heads turn in his direction. But unlike that morning, the cadets didn't seem scornful or pitying – they were looking at him with respect. He'd passed his first test.

# CHAPTER 3

**After lunch** the cadets donned helmets and body armour and boarded troop transports. On Lothal the instructors would have had to bark at everyone to calm down, but the Arkanis cadets found their seats with minimal conversation – clearly, a ride in a troop transport was nothing new to them.

*Yeah, but have any of you knocked one end over end with a thermal detonator?* Zare wondered, remembering how he'd foiled the Empire's pursuit of Beck Ollet's speeder in Lothal's Westhills, then had to flee the troop transport on his jumpspeeder. That had been the moment of no return – after that he'd been an insurgent, rebel, Separatist, or whatever the Empire called its enemies these days.

After a half hour the cadets disembarked and found themselves among lush green hills broken by patches of droopy shrubs. A clammy mist clung to them, and Zare removed his helmet to wipe irritably at the moisture beading inside his faceplate.

'Behold Arkanis's version of sunshine,' Penn said with a grin before closing his own faceplate. 'Come on, Leonis – our muster point's just over the hill.'

The cadets marched over a low rise. In a hollow beyond, instructors in grey Imperial Army uniforms were waiting next to a line of insect-like creatures. Each one was four metres long, with two parallel rows of legs on each side, an eyeless head that turned this way and that, and a wicked-looking barb on its hind-quarters. Saddles were attached to their backs, cinched tightly between segments covered by hard green plates.

A tall, hatchet-faced instructor was sitting atop one of the beasts. He jammed a prod between its segments, causing the creature to chitter and lash its stinger in protest.

'First time on a diplopod, Cadet Leonis?' the man asked. 'I'm Sergeant Pocarto. Don't worry – diplopods like their meat nice and rotten. Just don't make sudden moves if you're near their stingers. Now mount up, cadets.'

One of the instructors nodded at Zare, holding a diplopod's reins in one hand and a prod in the other. Zare put his hands uncertainly on the green shell. Beneath the chitin, the diplopod's innards rippled in a way that

Zare found faintly nauseating. He grimaced and hauled himself up into the saddle, then took the prod from the instructor.

'Kick it in the direction you want to go,' the instructor said. 'Both sides at once means go faster. If it gets ornery, poke it between the plates up by the head. It's an electro-prod, so don't touch the end.'

Zare kicked at the diplopod's sides and it reared up, emitting a wet-sounding gurgle that made the hairs on Zare's neck rise. But then it began to move forward, each segment rippling in turn and each pair of clawed legs hitting the ground together.

Anya kicked at her diplopod and brought the creature alongside Zare's mount.

'I'm your squad leader, Leonis,' she said. 'This is a scout mission, so we're a five-person unit – you, me, Manes, Harra, and Lanier. Harra's a rock – you can rely on her – but Manes gets overwhelmed under fire and tends to forget mission objectives. We all need to keep in contact with him – and reinforce the items from the briefing when we do.'

Anya started to swing her diplopod away.

'What about Lanier?' Zare asked.

Anya scowled. 'Don't waste time thinking about him – Xan Lanier's the worst cadet in the class.'

'He must have some potential. He's here, isn't he?'

'Forget Lanier – that problem will solve itself. He's here because somebody made a mistake. The commandant would rather see an Arkanis cadet wash out than become an officer who'll reflect badly on the Academy.'

Anya raised her foot to kick her diplopod, then reconsidered and turned back to Zare.

'This academy is for the best, Leonis,' she said. 'If you want to be the best, watch the company you keep. Don't waste your time with losers.'

Zare started to object, then nodded.

*Let it go,* he thought. *You're here to fight the Empire, not to worry about how it selects its officers.*

Zare knew the live-fire exercise was part of training cadets to enforce the Empire's will through military force. But it was still exhilarating. First his helmet's comlink crackled as a squad directed fire at targets on the ground, then gunships howled overhead, low enough that the air displaced by their passage shoved him lower in the saddle. Then the line of a missile streaked across the sky, blindingly bright, and he felt the ground shudder as a ball of fire rose from the impact site. The Arkanis cadets were brisk and efficient, coordinating advances and shifting formations with the confidence that came from extensive training.

'Close it up, Leonis,' Anya said in his ear. 'You should be fifty metres ahead of your current position.'

'Roger that,' Zare said. 'Having a little trouble controlling my diplopod.'

'You're doing great for day one,' Anya replied. 'Just be a little more aggressive with the prod.'

Zare jabbed his mount with the electro-prod, wincing when the creature recoiled from the spark and waved its head in agitation. But the beast picked up its pace.

'Lead, I'm pinned down here,' Lanier said. 'Request airstrike at 062-443.'

'That's a negative – all aerial units are spoken for,' Anya said. 'We'll have to proceed without you. Leonis, adjust your heading – I'll send updated course information to your HUD.'

'I have enemy units advancing on me!' Lanier objected.

'Lead, I can reinforce Cadet Lanier,' Zare said. 'We'll advance together.'

Static filled his ears.

'Did you copy, Lead?' he asked.

'I copy – they're jamming our channels,' Anya said, her voice distorted. 'It's too risky, Leonis. We can achieve our objectives with four units, but three is more problematic.'

'But I see the enemy units,' Zare said. 'I have a clear field of fire and can flank them. It'll only take a minute.'

'Is your helmet's heads-up display recording?' Anya asked.

'It is, Lead.'

'Then send the image from your HUD, Leonis,' Anya said reluctantly. 'I'll take a look.'

'Sent, Lead. Confirm reception?'

'Confirmed. Stand by. Okay, I've taken a look and – '

Silence. Zare smacked the side of his helmet, hoping to restore a loose connection.

'Lead?' he asked. 'Lanier, do you copy? Manes? Harra?'

No one replied. Communications were down.

Zare paused. Anya had seen the image from his helmet's camera. But what had she decided? He didn't know her well enough to guess.

*Anything you do is better than sitting here,* he thought. He decided to assist his fellow cadet. He kicked at his diplopod, hoping he wouldn't have to use the prod. The beast obediently turned to the left, and Zare put the prod in the sling beside his saddle, gripping the diplopod's sides with his knees and raising his blaster with both hands. He could see the trainers playing the role of the enemy ahead of him, advancing on a low ridge crowned with a scattering of large rocks.

Zare closed to twenty yards and began to fire. His volley of orange, low-intensity sting bolts hit the first trainer, who turned in Zare's direction and then lowered his blaster. Zare dropped a second trainer, forcing the rest of the enemy squad to seek cover. A sting bolt zipped by Zare's head and he kicked frantically at his diplopod, feeling horribly exposed atop the creature's back.

A sting bolt hit the diplopod's side, causing it to rear up in agitation. Zare's right foot slipped out of the stirrup and he dropped his rifle. He twisted in the saddle to grab it. That was a mistake – he tumbled off the diplopod, his nose smashing into the inside of his faceplate as he hit the ground. He scrambled to his knees, trying to get his bearings. A whistling noise overhead rose in volume until it became a shriek. He clutched his helmet and everything went black.

Zare blinked his eyes and saw nothing but bright green through his lenses.

Confused, he opened his faceplate. His gloves were dripping with green goo and his hands wouldn't stop shaking. His head was throbbing painfully.

He got to his feet, placing his hand on his diplopod's armoured side to steady himself. It felt strangely light. He looked at his mount and gasped. The diplopod had been blown in two – on the other side of the chitinous plates the ground was covered with green puddles surrounding mounds of slimy black and purple tubes.

Beyond what was left of the creature was a crater nearly ten metres in diameter, blasted into the top of the ridge. Smoke curled up from the pit. Zare looked into it and immediately turned away. At least Lanier hadn't suffered – he'd been killed instantly.

His comlink came to life, the channel filled with a babble of voices, including Anya's.

'Leonis! Report! Leonis!'

'I'm here,' Zare said. 'I'm all right. But . . . there's been an accident.'

'Lanier?' Anya asked.

'Yes. He's . . . he's dead.'

'Acknowledged. You're still showing status green, though. Advance to—'

'Advance?' Zare asked incredulously.

'This is still a live exercise, Leonis,' Anya said.

Zare couldn't believe it. A cadet was dead, and they were still going to play war?

'My mount's a casualty, too,' he said.

'So advance on foot. You'll need to double-time it.'

'Acknowledged, Lead,' Zare said, shaking his head at the madness of it all.

His blaster was half-buried in the dead diplopod's

innards. Grimacing, he fished it out of the mess and began to run.

When Zare got back to his troop transport, the other cadets stopped and stared. He didn't blame them – his grey field uniform was covered with goo, dry now but still brilliant green.

'Glad to see you're still in one piece, cadet,' said Pocarto. 'Though I think that uniform's a goner.'

'Is the inquiry when I get back, sir?' Zare asked. He didn't think he'd ever been so tired. Behind Pocarto, Anya was walking in Zare's direction, her helmet under one arm.

'DeeDee will let you know if more information about the accident is needed,' Pocarto said, clapping Zare on the shoulder and striding away. Zare watched him go, then turned to see Anya regarding him above crossed arms.

'Why did you ignore my order?' she demanded.

'I didn't,' Zare said. 'My comlink cut out, and I didn't know what you'd decided. I had to do something.'

Anya eyed him, her face hard, then nodded.

'All right. Don't worry about an inquiry – there won't be one.'

'But don't we need to know what went wrong?'

'We already do. A gunship copilot transposed

Lanier's coordinates with the strike coordinates. It wasn't any of our faults.'

Zare just stared at her.

'Who cares that it wasn't our fault?' he asked. 'One of our classmates is dead.'

'Mistakes get made in war,' Anya said coolly. 'And people die – the wrong ones along with the right ones, sometimes. And meanwhile, our class is stronger.'

That night, Zare was coming out of the bathroom when he nearly collided with a dozen cadets wearing field uniforms and helmets with closed faceplates. In the middle of them was Anya, bareheaded and puffy-eyed from sleep.

Zare took a step forward, thinking his squad leader was being blamed for the training accident. But one of the helmeted cadets intercepted him.

'Mind your business, Leonis,' he said, his voice harsh and metallic.

'It's all right, Zare,' Anya said. 'Go back to bed.'

Zare stepped aside to let the cadets pass. But there was no way he was going back to bed. He hurried into the dim barracks and yanked on his replacement field uniform, then rushed out into the corridor, boots in hand. At the entrance to the dormitory he crammed his feet into his boots and slipped outside into a chilly drizzle. The cadets were pale shapes crossing the lawn in the distance.

Zare hurried after them, crouching slightly, his boots squelching. The cadets were headed for the cliff and the trail that led down to the beach, he realised. He reached the edge of the lawn and crept a few metres along the stone path that zigzagged down the cliff, craning his neck to spot the cadets.

*The tower. They're going to the tower.*

Light flared below him, leaving spots on his vision. Something pale green shone on the beach, emitting sparks. Another light appeared in the darkness, briefly illuminating the first few metres of the causeway leading to the tower. The light pinwheeled through the gloom, shedding green sparks. Then two more of the strange torches were thrown from the beach, fizzing beneath the water just offshore. The wind changed and Zare wrinkled his nose at the acrid smell.

Below him, the cadets crossed the beach and began to walk across the causeway.

It was all he could do not to cry out when a hand fell on his shoulder, its grip cold and unyielding. Zare found himself staring into the black emptiness where DeeDee's face should have been.

'Cadets are not permitted out of their dormitories at night,' the droid intoned.

'They took Cadet Razar,' Zare said. 'I was afraid she was in trouble.'

'Cadets are not permitted out of their dormitories at night. You will be issued demerits.'

Zare took a last look back in the direction of the tower, then glumly followed DeeDee across the lawn.

The next morning, Anya was sitting at the commandant's table.

# CHAPTER 4

**Zare's demerits** appeared on his datapad at noontime – he was assigned to clean out the diplopod stables twice that week after dinner. But that was it – there was no other penalty and no order to explain his actions. Nor was there any hint of an investigation into the accident that had killed Xan Lanier. The Academy simply continued as if the luckless cadet had never existed.

But there was another level of activity that Zare noticed during every mealtime, classroom debate, and training exercise. Now that he knew who the Commandant's Cadets were, he kept seeing signs of connections among them. It wasn't just that they sat at the same table during meals. Three or four of them would come together for a moment on the lawn between classes, talking quietly before going their separate ways. Or one would answer a question of Julyan's and another would immediately reinforce the point, with nods exchanged among others scattered around the room.

On the second day after Lanier's death, Julyan began discussing counter-insurgency operations, running through a dizzying list of insurgent tactics seen in localised disturbances across the galaxy, from cell formation to coordination and blind message drops. Zare's eyes immediately jumped to Anya, and then to le Hivre, and over to Rav Horan.

*The Commandant's Cadets are like a cell – some kind of secret academy. But for what purpose?*

As Julyan walked them through an exploration of insurgents' recruitment techniques, Zare thought back to Lothal. Beck Ollet had witnessed stormtroopers brutally suppressing a peaceful demonstration by farmers angry that their lands had been polluted and despoiled. That had driven Beck to join a resistance cell, but he'd been captured and disappeared into Imperial custody. And Beck wasn't alone in resisting the Empire. While at Lothal's Imperial Academy, Zare had befriended a cadet he knew only as Dev Morgan, who turned out to be part of an insurgent band fighting the Empire.

Zare wondered if Beck and Dev's fellow insurgents had used the techniques Julyan was discussing. Had the two cells known about each other? Were they trying to create a larger anti-Imperial movement? Or were they both founded by Lothalites who'd been pushed too far and improvised, not understanding that the Imperial war machine was impossible to defeat?

But maybe the only way to achieve the impossible was to be unaware that was what you were trying to do.

After the afternoon's training exercise, the cadets emerged from the troop transports to discover the sun peeking feebly through the dirty grey clouds. Several cadets greeted the phenomenon with sarcastic applause.

'Cadets!' Pocarto barked. 'The commandant has declared an assembly in twenty minutes! Dress blacks and ceremonial sabres!'

'Does this happen every time the sun comes out?' Zare asked Rav Horan, who laughed and clapped him on the back.

Fifteen minutes later every cadet was standing on the lawn, showered and in the crisp uniform traditional for the Academy on Arkanis. Pocarto walked slowly among them, followed by DeeDee. The sergeant stopped in front of Zare and peered at his boots, examined the braid adorning his shoulder, then ordered him to present his sabre. Pocarto ran a white-gloved finger down the gleaming metal, then nodded.

'Someone trained you well, Leonis,' he said, and Zare offered silent thanks to Chiron and Currahee.

A sonic boom sent all the cadets' eyes skyward. A bat-winged Imperial shuttle emerged from the clouds, flying low over the grounds. But instead of landing on the platform in the middle of the lawn, it touched down atop the tower, wings inverted.

'Some muckety-muck's visiting,' Penn said from where he stood next to Zare. 'You need a serious security clearance to land at Area Null.'

'Is that what they call it? Area Null?'

Penn nodded.

'So what's in there?'

'Secret programs, they say. Anyone who knows isn't going to tell you. But if you believed everything you heard, you'd think the Emperor had a throne room in there.'

'So does he?' Zare asked, smiling to show he was kidding.

But Penn's face was grave. 'It's not something we talk about, all right?'

'There's a lot of that on Arkanis,' said Zare. As the cadets marched across the lawn, his eyes strayed to the black spike of the tower. His sister was in there – he was sure of it. And the only way he knew to get inside was to become a Commandant's Cadet.

* * *

The banquet hall was ancient, its stone ceiling supported by massive timbers of black wood. The cadets filed in, boot heels ringing on the stones, and stood in perfect lines before long tables. A single, smaller table stood atop a metre-high dais. That table had only a single occupant – a stocky man with red hair gone grey at the temples, and bright blue eyes.

'Present arms to Commandant Hux!' Pocarto shouted. Zare drew his ceremonial sabre, dipped it forward, paused with it held across his body, and then let it rest on his braided shoulder.

'At ease, cadets,' Hux said.

That night there was no commandant's table, Zare noticed. The cadets who'd won places in Hux's secret society were scattered among the others. Zare saw Anya looking in his direction. She smiled and he smiled back, only to see confusion in her eyes. Turning, Zare saw le Hivre seated at the table right behind him. Zare looked down, feeling his face flush. She hadn't been smiling at him after all.

The cadets began to murmur, looking up from the table and elbowing each other. Zare followed their gazes and froze.

DeeDee was leading the Inquisitor through the banquet hall. Zare's eyes tracked the grey-skinned Imperial agent as he made his way to Hux's dais and sat a couple of seats down from the commandant, with DeeDee standing between them behind their chairs.

Hux nodded at the Inquisitor and said something. The Inquisitor smiled in response, a baring of teeth that reminded Zare of a predator about to spring. The commandant spoke again, one finger raised for emphasis, and the Inquisitor scowled. They were arguing, Zare realised. He knew he should look away, but he couldn't. Was the Inquisitor there for him? For Dhara?

*Maybe it's something else entirely. Don't be paranoid.*

But a moment later, the Inquisitor's burning eyes turned Zare's way – and unlike with Anya, there was no doubt where he was looking. Those terrible eyes caught Zare's, and once again the Inquisitor smiled.

Zare looked away and forced himself to eat. But he barely tasted his food. The world had shrunk to himself and the being who had kidnapped his sister – and killed her, perhaps.

As the meal ended, DeeDee descended from the dais and clanked across the floor of the banquet hall. Zare simply watched as the jet-black droid grew closer and stopped, the faceless head pointed in his direction.

'Our guest requests your presence on the commandant's balcony,' DeeDee said.

The cadets around Zare had gone silent, their faces still and shocked.

'I—I don't know where that is,' Zare stammered.

'I shall lead the way.'

Zare followed Hux's droid up a narrow flight of stone steps. Ordinarily, the droid's deliberate pace would have annoyed Zare, but now DeeDee was moving entirely too quickly for his liking.

The Inquisitor was already there, standing in front of a parapet overlooking the grounds. It was raining again, but a stasis projector attached to the wall kept the Imperial agent dry.

'Welcome, Cadet Leonis,' the Inquisitor said, and as always his voice struck Zare as oddly beautiful – he sounded like a musician or a poet. 'Come out of the weather.'

As DeeDee departed, Zare forced his feet to carry him across the balcony to where the Inquisitor was waiting. Above them, the rain struck the stasis projector's cone and bounced away.

'I hear the commandant's machine prevented you from trying to enter Area Null,' the Inquisitor said, his eyes fixed on Zare. 'Tell me why you were there.'

'I—I thought my fellow cadet was in trouble. I wanted to help her.'

Those eyes flared bright, and Zare could almost feel the Inquisitor's anger boiling in the space between them.

'Don't you dare lie to me,' he growled, staring down at Zare. 'Commandant Hux has his own belief for why you wanted to get into the tower. I have mine. What were you doing, cadet? Did you sense something?'

'I did,' Zare said. 'Th—there's something in that tower that I'm meant to find. But I don't know what it is.'

He wondered if that was the right answer or a mistake that would expose him as a liar and leave him helpless before the Inquisitor's awful wrath. He was gambling again, pretending he could sense the strange phenomenon Dev Morgan had called the Force.

The Inquisitor began to pace, looking uncharacteristically agitated.

'Did Morgan ever mention the tower when you were on Lothal?' he demanded. 'Or something called Project Harvester?'

'No,' Zare said, trying to look baffled.

The Inquisitor stopped pacing and bared his teeth, taking a step in Zare's direction.

'Enough of this,' he growled.

Zare instinctively backed out of the stasis cone and into the rain. The sudden chill on his neck made him jump – as did the sight of DeeDee at the top of the stairs.

'Sir,' the droid said to the Inquisitor, 'I have a priority encrypted communication for you. From Lothal.'

The Inquisitor's eyes jumped to DeeDee, then back to Zare. He scowled but then mastered himself, placing his hands behind his back.

'It doesn't matter,' he told Zare calmly. 'Soon I will have Morgan and his deluded companions. And then all will be revealed, Cadet Leonis – whether you wish it or not.'

And then he strode away.

# CHAPTER 5

**'Cadet Leonis!** *Are you on the same planet as the rest of us?'*

Zare looked up in shock. Colonel Julyan was glowering down at him from his hovering lectern.

'No, sir. Sorry, sir. What was the question again, sir?'

Amid snickering from the other cadets, Julyan repeated his question about what the Imperial Navy might have done to counter the corsairs who were seizing pilgrims in the Metharian Nebula and delivering them to the Order of the Terrible Glare.

Fortunately, Zare had spent more than an hour the previous night studying that particular case file. It was exactly the kind of mission his younger self had dreamed of – a lawless group preying on innocent civilians and a chance for the Empire to restore order in a region plagued by chaos.

Julyan's face faded to a more reasonable colour as

Zare ticked off his proposed steps, and before Zare was finished he'd zipped back to the front of the classroom to sketch on the holographic display, eager to discuss the proper interdiction of hyperspace lanes.

Zare sighed in relief, then forced himself to give Julyan his full attention. He'd been trying to decipher clues about the Commandant's Cadets, wondering at the same time if every small sound of machinery indicated the Inquisitor had returned to Arkanis to confront him.

Neither was a useful way for him to spend his time. He couldn't control when the Inquisitor would return or what he would do when he did. All he could do was continue working to win a place in the commandant's secret society. And the way to do that was to pay attention – both in class and in the field. That was how he'd survived the Academy on Lothal, where enemies such as Captain Roddance and Cadet Oleg had tried to ruin him. And it was how he would survive Arkanis.

Or at least he hoped so.

Julyan was discussing the current trouble with smugglers and crime rings in the Minos Cluster, and Zare obediently called up the relevant node on his datapad, concentrating as summaries of reports from Imperial Intelligence filled the screen. They weren't dry academic records but actual intel delivered in real time. That was why the Arkanis cadets needed class-three clearance. The reports summarised fleet movements, informants' tips, arrest records, and more.

*Imagine what a group like Dev Morgan's could do with stuff like this. Or me, maybe. If I ever get Dhara out of here . . .*

He shook his head and listened carefully to Anya's question about interrogation. Daydreaming about some future that might never arrive was as useless as worrying about current perils he couldn't avoid. He could only focus on what was happening right then and hope it led, a moment at a time, to somewhere better.

On the third day after the Inquisitor's departure, the cadets had a rare free afternoon. Zare was staring down at the beach, trying to trace a strange knotty rope of black kelp, when Penn called his name.

'I'm going into Scaparus Port,' he said. 'Wanna come?'

'What's Scaparus Port?'

'It's a couple of klicks up the coast. Not much of a town but about all there is to do around here.'

Zare shrugged and nodded. Penn might be one of Anya's losers to avoid, but he was one of the few Arkanis cadets who'd been kind to Zare. And staring at the salt-rimed walls of Area Null wasn't going to do him any good.

They got a pair of diplopods from the stables and rode the ungainly creatures along a path that hugged the cliff, the coastline appearing and disappearing as the fog rolled across the rocky highlands and covered the mossy hills beyond. Zare's hair was stiff with salt within minutes.

'So why'd you want to join the Empire?' Penn asked.

'To make the galaxy a better place,' Zare said, reminding himself not to smile bitterly. That had been the dream of the boy he'd been when he'd stepped off a passenger liner on Lothal less than two years earlier.

'That's what I want, too,' Penn said.

Zare had to turn so he could hear the other cadet over the wind.

'I grew up on Syngia Station – Sertar sector,' Penn continued. 'It's a little place, doesn't even make all the registries of ports of call. My parents ran a depot there.'

'That was dangerous territory under the Republic,' Zare said.

'It still is,' Penn said. 'My parents weren't political. They stayed out of that stuff – said it was too big for little people trying to make a living.'

Zare said nothing, dreading what was coming.

'A gang of Zygerrian slavers docked at the station for emergency repairs on their hyperdrive,' Penn said, his voice flat. 'Nobody had a choice about it, but we thought it would be all right – they even paid for the repairs. Then, the morning they were due to leave, they must have changed their minds. They decided they couldn't leave witnesses. They took away everyone they thought might be worth something on Zygerria and killed the rest. I heard them coming and hid in a maintenance conduit.'

The wind whipped past and Zare heard the waves crashing against the rocks below them.

'Your parents?' he asked gently.

'I found out my mother died en route to Zygerria. My father didn't get that far. They decided he was too old. There was nothing I could do but hide.'

'I'm sorry, Penn.'

'I know you are, Zare – thank you. Trying not to get involved in galactic affairs offered my parents no protection. They needed a government that had the military might to protect them. The Empire wasn't strong enough to do that so far out in the Outer Rim back then, but I'm going to help make sure it can in the future. For my parents, of course. But not just for them – for other people's parents, too. So something like that can't happen again.'

They rode in silence, the diplopods rising and falling beneath them.

Zare looked over at Penn. He hoped the other cadet would get a chance to destroy pirates and slavers. But what would he do if his orders were to arrest peaceful protestors or drive farmers off their land? Or take children away from their parents?

If that happened, would Penn have to weigh the evil he might one day prevent against the evil he was perpetrating at the moment? And if he found that balance wanting, would he refuse an order? Or by then would he not even realise that he'd become a servant of evil – the very thing he'd once hoped to fight?

Scaparus was nestled in a gap in the cliffs, its stone and wood buildings crowned with yellow-and-green moss. The townspeople wore high boots and rough clothes, the colours muted by salt. Zare noticed that nearly all of them had some kind of fearful-looking injury – here an artificial forearm, there a line of deep sucker marks rising from a shirt collar to a missing eye.

'Fishing's a dangerous business on Arkanis,' Penn said quietly to Zare.

The town was divided between shops supplying fisherfolk and stores catering to cadets. Holographic signs promised sweets, self-heating caf, woollens, and other comforts. And nearly every shop boasted that it had a private comm booth.

'Aren't there comm booths at the Academy?' Zare

asked Penn as they handed the reins of their diplopods to a sad-eyed, feathered alien with clipped wings.

'There are, but Hux thinks contact with outsiders is detrimental to a proper military education, so you only get a fifteen-minute session once a month,' Penn explained. 'And supposedly DeeDee monitors the comm. So cadets come here. If you want to comm, go to Jasko's – it's right at the end of this street. And he's the only one who knows how to make a decent cup of caf.'

'And how do you know this Jasko doesn't listen in?'

'Jasko doesn't like Hux. Word in the barracks is he was a washout cadet and this is his way of getting even. Not to mention rich.'

The two cadets went their separate ways, with Zare cutting through a gloomy market where men and women of various species huddled under dripping canopies. Zare looked doubtfully at offerings of smoked fish and gnarled shellfish and was turning to leave when a splotch of bright purple caught his eye. A vendor was selling jogan fruit.

Zare bought a jogan with a sprig of blossoms still attached to its stem. He sniffed at the flowers and suddenly felt like he was standing in Beck Ollet's orchards on Lothal, surrounded by the sweetness of an autumn night.

He decided he'd visit Jasko's and comm his parents.

'Rememberin' home, young master?' the wizened fruit seller asked.

'Remembering friends,' Zare said, and smiled at her.

Auntie Nags's photoreceptors were red when she answered the comm terminal in the Leonises' apartment in Capital City, and the sight of Zare only made them fade to a reluctant yellowish orange.

'Zare Leonis!' the ancient nanny droid said. 'It's the middle of the night. Generally, one doesn't call after—'

'I'm glad to see you, too, Nags,' Zare said with a smile, waiting for the slight delay as his words were conveyed across the light years by hyperspace relays. 'The time's different on Arkanis. And this was my only chance to get away.'

'I hear your mother getting up, so I suppose what's done is done,' Nags said with a last flash of red photoreceptors. Then his mother was leaning close to the comm screen, her eyes wet. She held her hand up to the screen and Zare did the same, blinking away tears of his own.

'Oh, Zare, I'm so relieved,' Tepha Leonis said, and Zare knew at once that something was very wrong. His mother looked grey and haggard, and it wasn't just from being jolted awake in the middle of the night.

'Mum, what is it?' Zare asked, but then Tepha

looked to one side and Zare heard the clatter of his father crossing the room with the grace of the very recently awakened. Tepha bit her lip and moved aside so she could share the terminal with Zare's father, Leo.

'Son!' Leo said with a smile. 'How is Arkanis? I transferred liners there once – worst weather in the Outer Rim this side of Port Ferrule.'

Zare smiled and agreed, and he and his father bantered briefly about the horrible weather. At least, Leo noted, Arkanis's persistent rain wouldn't actually kill you. That could happen on worlds such as Lotho Minor and Gesaral Beta.

For Zare the conversation was simultaneously pointless and reassuring; whatever was wrong, it had nothing to do with his parents on Lothal. As Leo prattled on about agricultural test beds and various ministers' failings, Zare gave his mother a quick smile. Unlike Leo, she knew that the Empire's story about Dhara was a lie – just as she knew that Zare had entered Imperial service under false pretenses. But with Leo there, they could say nothing.

Leo finally ran out of news, and Zare said that he had to go. A long-range comm transmission wasn't cheap. They said their goodbyes – and then Tepha leaned close to the screen.

'You should talk to Merei,' she said.

Zare hesitated, remembering how he'd failed Merei. He wished he had a time machine or some other miraculous way of undoing his selfishness, but he didn't – and a middle-of-the-night comm from Arkanis wasn't going to help anything.

'It's important, Zare,' his mother said, her eyes fixed on his. 'Call Merei. Do it now.'

Tepha put her hand up to the screen. Then it went blank.

When Merei answered the comm her expression was as alarmed as Tepha's had been.

'Where are you?' she asked Zare.

'Arkanis. Not the Academy – a private comm-house.'

'Is it a secure feed?'

'The cadets here think so.'

He smiled as he watched her weigh that information. A moment earlier she'd been asleep, but now her brain was sifting through assumptions and possibilities, her calculations revealed in her pursed lips and the way she twirled her dark hair around one finger. She'd looked like that the first time he realised his affection for her was something deeper than friendship, back during study hall at AppSci. Zare stared at her, appalled that he'd ever let himself stop noticing things like that.

*Oh, Merei. I was such a fool.*

'I found out some things,' Merei said, leaning close

to her datapad and keeping her voice low. 'Your transfer to Arkanis wasn't a promotion, not really. The Inquisitor ordered it, in connection with his investigation of Dev Morgan. And because of Project Harvester.'

Zare nodded. So that was what had frightened his mother so badly – and rightly so. He didn't blame her. It terrified him, too.

'I figured that out already,' Zare said. 'The Inquisitor was here. He spoke to me.'

'What? When?'

'Three days ago. But then he was called back to Lothal suddenly. Merei . . . I know where Dhara's being held. She's in a tower, a part of the Academy called Area Null. With your access, I was hoping you could—'

He stopped. Merei was shaking her head, clearly frightened.

'My clearance won't do much good away from Lothal,' she said. 'It would raise security flags and—'

'All right, I understand. Forget it.'

That came out more harshly than he'd intended – he saw it in Merei's face.

'I mean, don't worry about it. It will be all right, Merei.'

'You don't know that. You *can't* know that.'

Zare said nothing. They looked at each other uncertainly for a moment.

'Well,' Zare said, 'I guess I better—'

But Merei had been saying something at the same time. They both stopped, waiting for each other, then tried to talk again at once, then stopped.

'You go first,' Zare said quickly. 'What were you going to say?'

'It's probably silly. I was going to ask you if you remember the smell of the jogan blossoms, the night Beck took us up into the Westhills.'

'I do. Of course I do. That's spooky – why did you ask me that?'

Merei hesitated, then offered him a small smile. 'It's kind of a long story. A poet told me about it.'

*A poet?* Zare wanted to laugh and started to say that it must be nice to be somewhere you could talk to poets. But he decided not to.

'Why is that spooky?' Merei asked.

'Because I just bought a jogan in the market. And it made me think of that same night.'

Merei smiled at him. Her eyes began to well up and she rubbed at them, embarrassed.

'I wish I could do more, Zare – I feel like I'm letting you down. Like I'm letting everybody down. It's just – the Empire's on the hunt. It's like they've gone crazy. They're investigating everything and everybody.'

'Well, I'm where I need to be,' Zare said, hoping that

a show of confidence he didn't feel might help her, too. 'I'm so close now, Merei. I know I am.'

But Merei just looked more alarmed.

'You're there because they *want* you there,' she said. 'The Inquisitor engineered this – for his own reasons. Which means you have to get out of there, Zare. Get off Arkanis and as far away as you can. Before he comes back.'

'And abandon Dhara?'

Merei looked at him helplessly, then hung her head.

# CHAPTER 6

**Two days** after Zare spoke to Merei, DeeDee appeared in the barracks as the cadets were preparing to head to the mess hall for dinner.

'All cadets report to the cliff edge, by order of the commandant,' the faceless black droid intoned, then strode out of the barracks as quickly as she'd appeared.

The cadets found Hux standing in the damp wind, staring out at the gunmetal-coloured sea with a boat cloak covering his uniform.

'At ease, ladies and gentlemen,' he said with a smile. 'We've got a juvenile nerf headed for the beach.'

Zare looked questioningly at Penn, who shrugged minutely.

'Follow me,' Hux said, then grinned. 'We won't tell DeeDee.'

The cadets followed Hux down the stone steps until the commandant stopped on a landing about halfway down the zigzag path and pointed below them at the rocky beach. Now Zare could see the nerf – a shaggy brown creature picking its way nervously down the last few steps. He put his hand over his mouth, trying not to laugh.

'What's so funny?' Penn asked.

'An Imperial commandant, fifty cadets, and one weird droid are watching a nerf climb down a staircase,' Zare said. 'It's a big galaxy, but I'm pretty sure that doesn't happen every day.'

Penn grinned, then erased the smile as Hux turned.

'Our nerfs are useful for keeping the lawns trimmed and weeded,' Hux said. 'Unfortunately, they come down here in search of salt – because they're incapable of learning what happens next.'

Hux went back to studying the beach. Zare watched the nerf snuffle at the rocks and snake out its long pink tongue to lick at them. Then one of the cadets pointed a few metres offshore, just beyond the waves. A thick black column was sticking out of the water, motionless.

'What is that?' Zare asked.

'Eyestalk,' said Rav Horan.

Then what Zare had assumed was kelp on the beach exploded into motion, wrapping the nerf up in dark muscular coils. The nerf bleated in terror as it was dragged into the water. Suckered tentacles erupted from the waves, attached to a wet black bulk that dragged itself through the shallows. A maw opened and the creature groaned. Then the nerf, the tentacles, and the eyestalk vanished beneath the waves, leaving a red slick on the water that quickly dissipated.

'And that's why aquatic sports aren't on the curriculum,' Rav said, to laughter from the other cadets. Zare just shook his head, appalled at the brutal speed with which the nerf's little life had been extinguished.

Hux turned and leaned against the balcony, eyeing the cadets.

'So, cadets: when you live next to a beach like this one, how do you stop your nerfs from being eaten?'

Tigard Manes's hand went up immediately, and Hux nodded at him.

'Put up a gate, sir,' he said. That was met with murmured laughter from a few of the other cadets.

'Very practical,' Hux said, and his eyes jumped to Zare. 'It would also keep out curiosity seekers.'

The commandant grinned, and Zare forced himself to nod in acknowledgement.

'But gates also delay those who have business on the other side of them. And we can't wall ourselves off from all the galaxy's dangers. So what's another way?'

Various cadets proposed drone monitors, shock fields, and other ideas that Hux rejected.

Then le Hivre raised his hand. 'Given enough time, sir, nature will solve the problem itself.'

'That's interesting, cadet. Explain how.'

Le Hivre smiled. 'Some nerfs like the taste of salt more than others. Those nerfs will be more likely to get eaten and less likely to reproduce. Within a few generations, you'll have a herd of nerfs that don't like salt. They won't go to the beach in search of it and won't get eaten.'

Hux rubbed his chin for a moment while le Hivre waited expectantly.

'I like that answer, cadet,' he said, and le Hivre brightened. 'But suppose we want to take a more active role than simply letting nature do its work.'

Zare raised his hand, and Hux nodded at him.

'Buy salt, sir. Give it to your nerfs.'

Hux cocked his head to the side, eyes narrowing. 'So you would coddle their weaknesses? Is that any way to create a strong herd, cadet?'

Several cadets around him chuckled, but Zare stood his ground. 'Better that than dead nerfs, sir.'

Hux grinned.

'A fair point, cadet,' he said. 'You can spend credits on salt or not, but it strikes me that the real answer to our problem is training. Train your nerfs that the beach means death. Punish them when they go near it, lest something else punish them.'

Now Anya's hand was up. Hux nodded at her.

'My last work assignment was caring for our nerfs, sir,' she said. 'It's only the juveniles that crave salt.'

'That's right,' Hux said. 'Which is why you have to train the herd from the very beginning. It's no good preparing to train a nerf at maturity if it never reaches that point.'

The commandant clapped his hands.

'Anyway, something to think about,' he said. 'You've done well here, and now you're ready for a true test – manoeuvres on Sirpar will begin in the morning. From your faces I can see some of you have heard of Sirpar. For the rest of you, know this: Sirpar is the forge where many an officer has been created – or broken.'

# CHAPTER 7

**Sirpar's gravity was** significantly stronger than standard, meaning every move Zare made on the hilly planet – from taking a step to lifting his blaster – made his muscles ache. The sun was a white dot so dazzlingly intense that the cadets were handed polarised goggles the moment they stepped off the landing craft. Even with eye protection, every shadow was strangely sharp-edged and the heat felt like a physical pulse.

The Imperial instructors assigned to the cadets' three-day tour were human but the product of generations on Sirpar. They were well shy of two metres in height but improbably broad and sheathed in thick layers of muscle. They didn't bark out orders, because they didn't need to – the cadets watched them carefully and jumped to obey their commands instantly. Or they would have if Sirpar's gravity had made jumping possible.

The cadets were stowing their gear when le Hivre appeared at Zare's side, wearing a major's rank badge.

'Red Battalion is my command. Rav's got Blue,' he said, eyes unreadable behind mirrored lenses. 'You're leading Cresh-3 Platoon, Leonis, with Cadet Cerroux as your sergeant major. Company Cresh is Anya's command.'

Zare nodded, but his mind was busy sorting through the Imperial military hierarchy he'd learned in his first days on Lothal: *Eight soldiers plus a sergeant make up a squad, four squads make up a platoon, four platoons make up a company, four companies make up a battalion.* If the Sirpar exercises featured two battalions, they had to include a lot more personnel than just the Arkanis cadets.

'So who are we commanding?' Zare asked.

'Stormtrooper units rotated off active duty for training,' le Hivre said.

'The troopers will take orders from cadets?'

'That's the value of discipline and training – to them we're officers. So act the part, *Lieutenant* Leonis.'

As Zare pinned his rank badge on to his field uniform, he thought of Ames Bunkle, his neighbour who'd entered the Academy on Lothal with Dhara. The last time Zare had seen Ames, the boy had barely recalled his own name, mechanically reciting his stormtrooper identification number instead.

That made Zare wonder about the soldiers he'd be commanding. Was it really training and discipline that led them to take orders from teenagers? Or had they been mentally bludgeoned into blind obedience to the Empire they served?

The first two days on Sirpar left Zare more tired than he'd ever been. At the conclusion of each day's training exercise, he and the other cadets trudged back to their barracks, struggling to lift their feet against the planet's relentless gravity, and even the relatively dim lights of the mess hall hurt Zare's eyes. From the faces around him, Zare knew the other cadets felt the same way. Penn was hollow-eyed with exhaustion, and even le Hivre looked pale and haggard, propping his chin up on both hands.

But Zare's platoon did well in exercises. Despite being veterans at least a decade older than he was, the troopers obeyed his commands instantly and fought effectively, responding to his orders with stoic nods and asking respectfully when something needed clarification. Both days his soldiers took positions, held their ground against 'enemy' assaults, and were always right where Anya needed them.

On the third day, Zare accompanied a squad in his platoon that was assigned to act as an artillery unit, holding a ridge carpeted in the knee-high, pale blue foliage common to that part of Sirpar. Zare peered through his electrobinoculars at the flatlands below, eyeing the enemy emplacement Anya's company needed to take.

'Fire another barrage – ground-penetrating missiles,' Zare said after double-checking the rest of his squads' positions. He tried not to think about the fact that his uniform was soaked through with sweat, or that his forearms ached from the simple act of holding up his electrobinoculars, or that when he closed his eyes he could still see the afterimage of his own shadow on his eyelids.

'Ground-penetrating ordnance it is, sir,' the trooper next to him said. 'Fire in the hole!'

Zare and the troopers ducked as the tripodal missile launcher coughed and the missile shrieked skyward. Zare dragged the electrobinoculars back up to his eyes and stared at the bunker below. The missile impacted with a flash in the air a few metres above the bunker. For training exercises the Empire used dummy warheads programmed to explode before actually reaching their targets.

*Or at least that's the way it's* supposed *to work,* he thought darkly, remembering how Xan Lanier had died.

'Perfect shot,' Zare said, and waited for one of the instructors to estimate the damage that an actual ground-penetrating missile would have done.

But when the assessment crackled over his comlink he scowled. 'Target's better armoured than we thought,' he told his squad. 'But we're softening them up, so—'

'I have gunships incoming!' yelled Cerroux as Zare's comlink filled with alarmed warnings.

'Get down!' Zare told the troopers. 'Cover that launcher!'

His shoulders and legs screamed for relief as he scrambled across the top of the hillside, scraping his cheek on the spiny edge of a tough, bladelike Sirparian leaf. He flung himself into one of the cramped dugouts his troopers had prepared that morning, squinting and trying to spot the gunships overhead against the brilliant sun. Before he could see them, the sky flared into a sheet of white. When Zare opened his eyes he saw nothing but purple spots and his head was screaming.

'Red-Cresh-3-1, this is Training Central,' someone with a thick Sirparian brogue said in his ear. 'You've taken no casualties, but that electro-proton blast fried your communications and your artillery launcher.'

'Acknowledged, Central,' Zare said unhappily. He

looked around and saw the collapsed launcher lying half in and half out of one of the dugouts. The soldier firing it hadn't quite gotten it under cover in time.

'Got caught in the underbrush, sir,' he said apologetically from behind his white helmet.

'Run a diagnostic check,' Zare said. 'See if we can restart it.'

The answer was no. Still blinking away spots, Zare gazed down at the bunker below them. He half-wished his squad had been ruled casualties. That would have been a failure, but at least they could have sprawled in the dugouts until the next exercise.

*But that didn't happen, cadet. So figure out what to do instead.*

'Trooper, is your ordnance still operable?' he asked.

'Launcher's fried, sir.'

'I know that. I'm talking about the projectiles themselves.'

'They're live, sir. But ain't got no way to deliver them. Unless we carry them down there ourselves.'

Zare nodded, grimacing at the ache the motion caused in his neck.

'That's exactly what we're going to do. Squad, skirmish formation. Divide up the ordnance. Bedal, use flash code to tell Captain Razar our plan. Then signal the other squads.'

But Cerroux looked at him in disbelief.

'Our orders are to occupy *this* position,' he said.

'Without artillery, *this* position is useless,' Zare snapped, aware of the troopers' watching the argument. 'Our target is down there. Which means our missiles need to be down there.'

'They'll pick us off like nerfs,' Cerroux complained. 'It'll hurt our scores in the exercise.'

'The company will meet its objectives – that's the only thing that matters, cadet,' Zare said. 'Now let's move.'

Cerroux affixed his flasher to his blaster and began blinking out the message. Zare just hoped Anya and the other squads would see it.

When the signals had been sent, Zare crammed a missile into his own backpack and got to his feet, gritting his teeth at the pain in his shoulders and legs.

'It's nearly a klick to the bunker,' he told the troopers. 'Don't exhaust yourselves trying to cover the distance all at once. But keep moving – don't let them zero in on your position.'

He started down the hill, the sharp leaves raking his legs. Sweat was pouring down his face, getting behind his polarised goggles and dripping in his eyes.

Orange sting bolts began to fly out of the bunker when they'd gone two hundred metres. Zare lost three troopers within a minute and was nearly hit himself when he paused to yell for the survivors to spread out. Another trooper was dropped by enemy fire when they were still three hundred metres from the bunker.

*'Watch for skirmishers!'* Zare screamed, his tongue thick in his mouth and his lungs aching. *'Go! Go! Move it, troopers!'*

Two hundred metres to go. Red-Cresh-3-1 had just two troopers left, plus himself. He tripped over a root and landed on his face in the dirt, then crawled forward until he could force his body upright again. He was gasping for air and could barely see.

One hundred metres. A trooper from Blue Battalion charged around the bunker. Zare shot him before he could bring his E-11 up. But another soldier firing from cover hit one of Zare's last two troopers.

*'Activate ordnance! Ten-second timer!'*

Zare fought to get free of his backpack, flinging it in front of him with an effort that sent agony through his shoulder. He snatched up the pack, pulled out the missile inside, and tapped at the keypad set in its base. A sting bolt zipped past his ear with a shrill chirp. Then Zare and his lone remaining trooper were against the wall of the bunker, gasping for breath. The timer hit zero and the trooper nodded at Zare.

'We got 'em, sir. Scratch one blue bunker.'

'Red-Cresh-3-1, your target is destroyed,' an instructor said in Zare's ear. 'And so are you.'

Zare lay in the shadow of the bunker, unable to move. The troopers who'd already been eliminated by simulated fire trudged toward him.

'At ease, boys,' Zare said, indicating the shade around him with an exhausted smile. 'Seeing how we're dead and all.'

The *Sentinel*-class landing craft taking the cadets back to Arkanis felt like it had been sent from paradise. It was cool and dim, and the standard gravity made Zare feel like he was floating. He fell asleep in moments, only to be awakened by a hand gently shaking him.

'Relax, Leonis,' le Hivre said in a low voice. 'Come with me.'

He led Zare back to the passageway by the head and medical station.

'You did well back there. Anya says our mission would have failed without your bit of improvisation,' le Hivre said. 'So are you ready for a more serious commitment? One that's invitation only?'

'I am,' Zare said, trying to keep his voice steady.

'Good. But that's the easy part. Are you willing to prove it? To show you'll do anything to help create a stronger Empire?'

Zare nodded.

'You'll hear from us in a day or two, then,' le Hivre said. 'But understand this, Leonis: the demonstration won't be simulated.'

# CHAPTER 8

**As he'd feared,** someone was expecting Zare when the cadets returned to Arkanis. But it wasn't the Inquisitor.

CONGRATULATIONS ON SURVIVING SIRPAR, the message on his datapad read. ASSUMING I HAVE NOT DROWNED OR BEEN DEVOURED BY SOME SORT OF PREDATORY MOSS BY THEN, PLEASE REPORT TO MY NEW OFFICE HERE ON ARKANIS DURING YOUR FIRST FREE PERIOD IN THE MORNING. WITH ALL REGARDS, LT. CHIRON.

Zare stared at the message in wonder. What was the Imperial officer who'd served as his mentor on Lothal doing on Arkanis?

When Zare found his way to Chiron's office, he saw that the lieutenant had barely unpacked. Zare smiled at him but felt torn. Chiron was a decent man, and Zare was genuinely glad to see a friendly face – yet deceiving

Chiron on Lothal had been painful and abandoning that charade had been a relief.

'Cadet Leonis reporting as ordered, sir,' Zare said. 'Have you been transferred here as well, sir?'

Chiron looked surprised. 'You haven't heard, then? Oh – but of course you wouldn't have. You've been on manoeuvres. You'd better sit.'

Zare settled into his chair, listening to the rain beat on the office windows. For once Arkanis's cool wet weather and muted colours came as a relief.

'I suppose you'll hear eventually anyway,' Chiron said, his expression serious. 'Commandant Aresko and Taskmaster Grint were . . . relieved of command. Personally, by Grand Moff Tarkin. Captain Roddance is temporarily in charge of the Academy on Lothal.'

Zare couldn't suppress a scowl at the name of the brutal Imperial whose troops had killed peaceful protestors in the Westhills and who had ordered the Lothal cadets to take children into custody.

'And let me guess – the first thing he did was transfer you, sir,' he said, knowing Chiron disliked Roddance, too.

Chiron tried to look disapproving, but his eyes were warm with amusement.

'He wasn't sad to see me go, let's put it that way. And poor Sergeant Currahee is in a state. But that's not the reason I'm here. Major Cass, aide to Governor Tarkin, transferred me here to investigate a confidential matter.'

When Zare looked questioningly at Chiron, the handsome lieutenant leaned forward, eyes fixed on Zare.

'Can you keep a secret, Cadet Leonis?'

Zare nodded, thinking that Chiron would be shocked by some of Zare's secrets.

'Talk is that Commandant Hux has created a secret society within this academy, made up of handpicked cadets. Have you heard anything about that, Cadet Leonis?'

Zare couldn't keep the surprise off his face. He ducked his head and looked away, out at the fog-enveloped grounds.

If he told Chiron what he knew, perhaps the lieutenant could get him inside Area Null. On the other hand, acknowledging Chiron's suspicions might disrupt Hux's society, keeping Zare out of the tower he desperately needed to get into.

'Why would a Grand Moff be interested in what's happening here?' Zare asked, stalling for time.

'Commandant Brendol Hux is a man who inspires strong loyalties,' Chiron said. 'The Empire depends on a clear chain of command, and loyalties independent of that chain of command are potentially dangerous. Right now, my job is to investigate – nothing more. So have you heard anything or not?'

'I'm sorry, sir, but you're putting me in a difficult position,' Zare said. 'If you give me a day or two, I might be able to help you more than I can now.'

Chiron nodded.

'I think I understand – and I trust you to make the right decision about bringing me into your confidence. I'll wait for word from you, Cadet Leonis.'

Zare nodded and got to his feet but hesitated when Chiron extended a gloved hand for him to shake.

'Sir? One question, if I may: did anyone come with you from Lothal?'

'No. I came alone. What's wrong, Zare?'

'The Inquisitor was here, sir,' Zare said, hesitating as the blood drained from Chiron's face. 'Before Sirpar. But he was called away to Lothal.'

Chiron turned away.

'What I'm going to tell you, cadet, is top-secret information,' he said. 'The Inquisitor is dead – killed by insurgents with connections to Lothal.'

Zare looked at him in shock.

'I assure you it was an isolated incident,' Chiron said. 'There's no danger to your parents, or to anyone else on Lothal.'

Zare thanked him and left the office, barely registering the chilly rain. The Inquisitor wasn't coming back to Arkanis that day, or ever. The being who had ordered Dhara's kidnapping was dead.

Zare felt like a weight pressing down on him had been removed. But the relief was short-lived. He knew the Empire had many servants – and someone worse might arrive to take the Inquisitor's place.

# CHAPTER 9

**That night a** vicious storm lashed the Academy and a lightning strike knocked the feeds from the power plant offline, plunging the buildings into darkness. Zare drifted in and out of sleep as lightning left the barracks alternately pitch-black and starkly lit, and he thought he was dreaming when he woke up to find his bunk surrounded by figures in black cloaks.

Realizing he was awake, he panicked, convinced that Chiron was mistaken and the Inquisitor had sent for him. But it was his fellow cadets, dressed in foul-weather gear. One held a finger up to his faceplate and Zare nodded, then dressed silently and followed the little group out into the driving rain.

He hoped they were heading for Area Null, but their destination was the darkened banquet hall.

Once inside, the cadets lowered their hoods and opened their faceplates, revealing the faces of the

Commandant's Cadets. Le Hivre stepped forward, smiling thinly.

'You've been accepted for initiation into our ranks, Zare Leonis,' he said. 'But now you must prove yourself worthy. This academy prides itself on the quality of its graduates – but the way we ensure that quality is by weeding out the weak ourselves.'

Le Hivre nodded at Anya, who stepped forward and pulled an E-11 blaster rifle out from under her cloak. Zare took it, looking at her in confusion.

'It'll happen in the field manoeuvres three days from now,' Anya said. 'Use this during the exercise. You and your target will be on different sides – it's all been arranged. Engage and disengage the safety three times in a row and your E-11 will fire full-intensity bolts. Don't worry – you'll be cleared without an inquiry. It'll be just a slight weapons malfunction.'

Zare looked at her in astonishment. Xan Lanier's death hadn't been an accident, and no gunship pilot had been at fault. Anya had killed him – and nearly Zare as well – to earn her place among the Commandant's Cadets.

'Who's the target?' he asked, hoping his voice sounded cold.

'Penn Zarang,' le Hivre said. 'He's not the bottom of the class, but no one thinks he'll be able to pull up his marks, and he's not Arkanis material. Eliminate him and you'll be one of us.'

Zare knew he looked shocked, because le Hivre's eyes narrowed and he crossed his arms over his chest.

'On Sirpar you had to make sacrifices for the good of the Empire and didn't hesitate, Leonis. Now you'll do it for real. Or is your dedication only pretend?'

Zare stiffened in the mess hall when Penn sat down next to him, and he responded to the other cadet's morning chatter with shrugs and monosyllables. It was monstrous to think of killing a fellow cadet in cold blood – particularly one who'd been kind to him.

But what if he refused to carry out le Hivre's orders? He'd never become a Commandant's Cadet, which was the only way he knew to get into Area Null. The Inquisitor was dead, but he couldn't imagine the Empire would shut down Project Harvester and free his sister. Instead, he knew, Dhara and any other subjects of the Inquisitor's program would disappear – as so many victims of the Empire had.

Or perhaps the program would continue. Perhaps there were other Inquisitors – ones who might even now be reading their predecessor's files and wondering about the name Zare Leonis.

As the day went on Penn seemed to be everywhere.

He was the one answering questions in Julyan's class and the cadet next to Zare when Pocarto inspected them in a driving rain, taking umbrage at Zare's scuffed boots. And Penn was designated as part of blue team when Zare's red team advanced too quickly to take a position.

The rain was fogging their helmet lenses, so the cadets on both red and blue teams were training with their faceplates open. Zare was reloading his E-11's power pack when Penn popped up from behind an outcropping, his own blaster raised.

'Sorry, Zare,' he said, and hit his fellow cadet in the chest with a sting bolt.

Zare grunted as the bolt sent burning sensations down his arms, making his fingers spasm. A bell-like tone tolled in his ear, signalling that he was ineligible to continue the simulated fight. Penn offered him a grin and a salute as Zare trudged off to wait with the other eliminated cadets. Normally, Zare would have returned the salute but not that day – because in two days they'd meet and the encounter would end in a horribly different fashion.

*Penn's not my friend*, he thought. *He's training to be an Imperial officer – to be everything I've fought against.*

But as far as Zare knew, Penn had never done anything to harm anyone. He'd entered Imperial service because he wanted to prevent what had happened to his parents from happening to anyone else. But for a quirk of fate, the two of them might have found their roles reversed.

*I've done things I'm not proud of,* Zare thought. *But never anything like what I'm being asked to do now.*

The thought made his stomach turn. What if he saved his sister's life but spent the rest of his days remembering that he'd taken Penn's? He didn't think he'd be able to live with himself for making that trade.

But the alternative was to refuse, knowing it would be a death sentence for his sister. And how could he live with himself if he did that?

# CHAPTER 10

**The next morning,** Zare skipped breakfast and hurried across the lawn, grateful that the fog hid him from any watching eyes. Unable to wait a moment longer, he broke into a run, water flying around his boots, and then rushed up the stairs to Chiron's office.

The lieutenant was at his desk, hands around a warm mug of caf.

'I'm not a murderer,' Zare said. 'I won't do it.'

'A murderer? What's this about?'

As Chiron listened in grave silence, Zare told him about the Commandant's Cadets and the accident that had killed Xan Lanier, and about what he had been told to do.

'This stops now,' Chiron said, his handsome face pale with anger. 'I can cross-reference the names of the Commandant's Cadets with training accidents and other incidents.'

'If those records haven't been falsified,' Zare said. 'After Cadet Lanier died there wasn't even an inquiry.'

'True,' Chiron said, scowling. 'I need more information. My code cylinder gives me access to Area Null – Major Cass arranged that – but that's worthless if I don't know what's happening inside.'

*I need to know that, too,* thought Zare, but he shook his head.

'I can't do it, sir,' he said. 'I *won't*.'

'I think I know how we can do this without anyone dying,' Chiron said. 'Does Cadet Zarang trust you?'

Zare nodded miserably.

'Good. Two hours after lights out, bring him to the edge of the woods, by the diplopod pen.'

'DeeDee will catch us,' Zare objected.

'I'll arrange a special assignment for DeeDee,' Chiron said. 'All you have to do is be there. Leave the rest to me.'

Later that night, Penn's eyes went wide at the sight of Zare standing beside his bunk, dressed in his field uniform.

'Not a sound,' Zare whispered. 'Not if you want to live.'

The red-haired cadet dressed quickly, with Zare wincing at each sound he made, and the two stole out of the dormitory and across the dark campus. Despite Chiron's assurances, Zare kept waiting for DeeDee to materialise out of the fog, bringing recriminations and demerits.

But Zare and Penn reached the diplopod pen without incident and found a figure in a dark cloak waiting for them. At the figure's feet were three shovels and a bag, heavy with something that made Zare want to hold his nose.

'You're the new lieutenant,' Penn said when Chiron drew back his hood. 'What is this, sir?'

Chiron looked at Zare, whose mind jumped back to the night on Lothal when he and Dev Morgan had spirited Jai Kell out of the barracks to tell him he was in terrible danger.

'You've been marked for death by the Commandant's Cadets, Penn,' Zare said. 'I'm supposed to kill you.'

Penn's eyes jumped to the tall figure of Lieutenant Chiron and the shovels. He took a step back, eyes wild.

'Nothing bad is going to happen, cadet,' Chiron said.

'Why me?' Penn demanded. 'There are cadets with lower marks than mine!'

'I don't know,' Zare said. 'But it's you.'

'Wh—what's in that bag?' stammered Penn.

'Side of nerf,' Chiron said. 'It went bad when the freezer cut out in the storm the other night. It's going to be a stand-in for your body while you're on a transport for somewhere else.'

'No!' Penn said, and Zare looked around in alarm. 'This is crazy!'

'Penn, think,' Zare urged. 'If I refuse, either they'll kill both of us or someone else will get invited to join them. Someone else will get the order to demonstrate their loyalty. Only that cadet won't tell you it's coming. If you stay here, you'll die.'

Penn looked wildly from Zare to Chiron.

'But you can stop this, sir!' he said.

'That's what I'm doing,' Chiron said. 'And our little ruse is part of that. But I can't stop it tonight.'

'It's not fair,' Penn said. 'I want to be an Imperial officer! I want to serve the Emperor!'

'Cadet Leonis told me you might say that,' Chiron said. 'Listen to me, Zarang. Lay low until my investigation is over and I'll figure out how to get you a transfer to another academy. I'll raise your case with Governor Tarkin himself if I have to.'

Penn looked questioningly at Zare.

'You can trust him,' Zare said.

Penn hesitated, and Zare blew out his breath in

exasperation. 'It would have been a lot less risky to kill you, you know.'

Penn nodded slowly and reached out to take a shovel from Chiron.

# CHAPTER 11

**The buzz** spread quickly through the barracks the next morning. Cadet Zarang was missing, and he wasn't on the sick list, either.

Zare said nothing, but on his way to the showers a hand landed heavily on his shoulder and he turned to see le Hivre staring at him, red spots of fury on his cheeks.

'You warned him,' he hissed. 'You're finished, Leonis.'

'Warned him?' Zare said coolly. 'Hardly. I *killed* him. Last night.'

Le Hivre looked astonished.

'Zarang had done enough to pull down our class already. Why blemish my training record?' Zare asked. 'I'll take you to the grave myself.'

'You'd better,' le Hivre said, and stalked off.

Zare, le Hivre, and Anya all had free periods after their mid-morning training exercise. The two Commandant's Cadets followed Zare past the diplopod pen and about twenty metres into the woods, to an area of disturbed dirt surrounded by boot prints.

'He's in there?' le Hivre asked. 'You're lying. Dig it up. Show me.'

'No,' Zare said, leaning against a tree. 'I already did the dirty work. You want to dig, do it yourself. But it won't be pleasant – stuff decays awful fast here on Arkanis.'

Le Hivre looked uncertainly at Zare, then nodded at Anya. The two Commandant's Cadets removed their belts and holsters, found fallen tree limbs, and began to scratch awkwardly at the dirt while Zare watched, trying not to let his anxiety show. The two cadets dug for two minutes, then three as the rain began to fall.

*If they find the nerf I'll have to shoot them,* Zare thought. *Pump the safety three times and I'll be firing full-intensity bolts.*

And then what would he do? He didn't know. Perhaps he should tell Chiron everything and appeal to him for help.

*One crisis at a time,* Zare thought.

'I hit something,' Anya said, and le Hivre peered into the hole.

'It's a cadet's jacket,' he said, glancing at Zare, then back at Anya. 'Keep digging.'

Anya put both hands on her stick and pushed – and a moment later a dreadful stench sent her reeling away from the hole. Le Hivre stepped hastily away from the grave and Zare's stomach lurched.

'I quit,' Anya said, hurling her tree limb aside and giving Zare a look that was equal parts horror and admiration.

'We could get a construction droid,' le Hivre said. 'To find out for sure.'

'Do what you want,' Anya said. 'Julyan's class begins in fifteen minutes and I'm not getting a demerit for being late.'

Le Hivre frowned, looking from the disturbed earth to Zare. But then he nodded.

'You're more ruthless than I'd guessed, Leonis,' he said. 'Welcome to the Commandant's Cadets.'

Following the afternoon training exercise, Rav Horan pulled Zare aside and told him the Commandant's Cadets were dining with Hux. Zare nodded and put on his black dress uniform, ignoring the sideways looks and whispers in the barracks.

Hux was sitting in a pool of light at the head of a single table in the banquet hall, with DeeDee at his side. The table had another twelve place settings. Hux told the cadets to sit, and as the newest Commandant's Cadet, Zare found himself at Hux's right elbow, across from Anya.

'The addition of Cadet Leonis will complete our ranks,' Hux said. 'All of you have proved yourselves exemplary servants of the Empire, destined to become champions of a stronger galactic order. Now it's time for you to learn of our ultimate purpose.'

The banquet hall was silent – those cadets who'd been eating were now sitting with utensils motionless in their hands. DeeDee turned her blank faceplate to survey the table.

'During the Clone Wars, I served in the Grand Army of the Republic,' Hux said. 'I was a junior officer who communicated tactics and strategy as determined by our Jedi generals.'

The cadets sat in stony silence, disturbed by what they knew was a forbidden subject.

Hux chuckled.

'Come now, ladies and gentlemen,' he said. 'The Empire has nothing to fear from the tattered remnants of an extinct cult. But I mention the Jedi because we can learn from them – as we must learn from all our enemies.'

Hux got up from his chair, gesturing impatiently for the cadets to remain seated. He began to pace, with DeeDee's head carefully tracking her master's progress.

'The Republic's clones were effective soldiers because they weren't just trained for battle but *bred* for it,' Hux said. 'Their training began at birth, with newborns tested for eyesight and reflexes. You've all learned that. But what you may not know is that the Jedi were the same way – they searched the galaxy for babies and young children who shared their sorcerous gifts and trained them from the cradle. In both cases, the result was a cadre of superior, fanatically loyal warriors.'

Zare stared at Hux. Was that why the Inquisitor had taken Dhara? To turn her into a warrior loyal to some new philosophy? And did Hux's talk of the Jedi mean he was involved in Project Harvester, as well?

'The clones' nature posed a weakness, however,' Hux said. 'Because they were genetically identical, they were vulnerable to the same biological agents and pathogens – and, indeed, Separatist scientists spent much of the war seeking to create bespoke viruses that would target the clone armies.

'Our Emperor was aware of this possibility and

opened the ranks of the military to the entire galactic populace. By doing so, he avoided the clones' genetic vulnerabilities and ensured that Imperial citizens knew their military was made up of their own families, rather than some lesser order of humanity. But there was a trade-off – with the clones trained from birth to be soldiers, no non-clone could ever equal their prowess in battle.'

The cadets turned in their chairs to watch the commandant's relentless pacing.

'But what if there were a way to avoid that trade-off?' Hux asked. 'What if you could train non-clone soldiers from birth? Isn't that exactly what the Jedi did?'

The commandant stopped behind his chair and rested his hands on it, his brilliant blue eyes fixing on each cadet in turn.

'We can train stormtroopers from birth, as the clones and Jedi were,' he said. 'Over generations, through careful observation and selection, we will create an army that has all the clones' strengths but none of their weaknesses. Stormtroopers utterly loyal to the Empire who see it as their family – because that is what it will be.'

Hux smiled, smacking the back of his chair for emphasis.

'This has been a dream of mine for years,' he said. 'I searched for officers who would understand what I proposed, and who could help me create these champions of our Empire. When I didn't find those officers, I decided to follow my own advice – *I would create them.* You have been chosen to begin this great work alongside me – to execute my design. Together, my cadets, we shall oversee the creation of legions that ensure the Empire lives forever.'

The cadets began to cheer. Zare joined them, a sickly smile plastered to his face, then forced himself to eat – to cut his meat and raise his glass and answer Hux's questions. He was so close now. He must not betray the slightest sign that he was anything other than absolutely committed to Hux's mad scheme.

Droids appeared to clear the tables, and Hux seized Zare's wrist in an iron grip.

'And now we have a new cadet to initiate,' the commandant said.

The cadets followed Hux across the lawns, with DeeDee at their rear. One of Arkanis's moons had risen, turning the coastal fog into a bright blur and the tower into a black spike in silhouette.

The cadets walked down the stone steps to the beach. Zare heard the waves below them in the darkness. His heart was beating hard and he blew out his breath, trying to calm himself.

Two of Hux's cadets ignited flares, then tossed them onto the rocky beach and into the shallow water. Zare wrinkled his nose at the smell, trying to ignore the wet scrabbling sounds in the darkness around them.

They were on the causeway now, the tower a looming shadow above them. On either side the black water churned.

'And halt,' Hux said. Zare waited with the others in the darkness. There was a muffled clang and the tall metal doors to the tower opened, leaving the cadets blinking in the sudden light.

They marched inside. Zare looked around, trying to take stock of his surroundings, aware that he was closer to his sister than he'd been since he last saw her on Lothal. A guard station stood ahead of them, in front of a bank of elevators and corridors leading deeper into the tower. On either side, broad doorways led to stone steps heading upward.

The officers seated behind the consoles got to their feet, saluting. One officer walked over and spoke quietly to Hux.

'One moment, cadets,' Hux said. 'Another group is finishing a bit of business in our ceremonial room.'

The cadets stood in two lines, waiting. Zare heard

the sound of feet heading in their direction. A line of boys and girls about the same age as the cadets emerged from the right-hand corridor, marching toward them. They wore orange jumpsuits.

'Project Unity,' Hux said. 'Former dissenters who have reconsidered their errors and rededicated themselves to the Imperial cause.'

There was something faintly disturbing about the boys and girls in orange uniforms – they were glassy-eyed, with blank expressions. Zare wondered if they'd been brainwashed, drugged, or both.

His eyes passed over a boy near the end of the line, then leapt back to his face.

*No. No, no, no. It can't be. IT CAN'T BE.*

But it was.

Beck Ollet was marching toward him.

Zare turned his head away, pretending to study something on the stone wall. But Beck had stopped. He shook his head, confused. Then his eyes widened.

His arm rose and he pointed directly at Zare.

# PART 2:
# MEREI

# CHAPTER 12

**When Tepha Leonis** finally let go of Merei, her eyes were red and streaming – and Merei knew she didn't look much better herself. But she'd thought Tepha needed to know what she'd discovered in the Imperial records: that Zare, who'd left earlier that day for Arkanis, had been transferred there as part of the same secret program that had ensnared his sister, Dhara, and because the Empire suspected there was a connection between him and the recent insurgent activity on Lothal.

Merei promised Tepha that she'd let her know anything she heard, then sped away on her jumpspeeder. But something else was bothering her besides Zare's departure.

One of Merei's jobs for the ambitious young criminal Yahenna Laxo had been to keep tabs on the fugitives, dissidents, and other unfortunates paying Laxo to hide them in bolt-holes across Capital City.

Laxo was now dead, killed by stormtroopers in a confrontation Merei had engineered in a desperate effort to free herself from his clutches – a confrontation that had ended with the troopers' opening fire instead of arresting her boss as she'd expected.

Before he'd died, Laxo had ordered her to take a bounty hunter to the hideout used by Holshef, an elderly poet branded a dissident by the Empire. Fortunately, Merei hadn't needed to keep that appointment. But what had happened to Holshef?

She pulled her jumpspeeder over to the side of the road, earning a horn blast from a droid speeder truck.

'*Wox ho uffdon comda,*' the truck squalled at her.

'To you too,' she said, adding a casually rude gesture.

Merei knew she'd been extremely lucky to escape Laxo's clutches and her own mother's investigation into the data breach Merei had caused at the Transportation Ministry. Either could have landed her in prison. To put herself in further danger felt like wasting her second chance, and she knew it was madness to think she'd get a third.

But could she really leave Holshef to be turned out of his hiding place? The thought of the gentle old poet in Imperial custody made her sick.

Merei sighed and gunned her jumpspeeder, earning herself another reprimand from a different droid truck. She headed for the south side of Capital City and its industrial quarter. The address where Merei hoped Holshef was still hiding – 1044 Chapel – looked like half a dozen of the neighbouring buildings on its block. It was a low-slung warehouse built of adobe and expanded with synthetic stone.

Merei slowed her jumpspeeder and circled the block, ready to race off if she spotted someone getting out of a parked vehicle, a drone in the sky, or some other sign that she was being watched. But there was nothing. She parked her bike, tried to wipe the dust from her face, and thumbed the warehouse's buzzer.

A male voice grumbled something in a language she didn't know, then stopped and started over.

'You're the Syndicate's kid courier,' he said.

That was reassuring on one hand but alarming on the other. Merei licked her lips, reminding herself that as Laxo's agent she hadn't been in the habit of taking poodoo from anybody – even if that somebody was bigger and meaner and carrying a blaster.

'Open up – we need to talk,' she said, and a moment later the door opened.

A Lutrillian emerged from the depths of the warehouse, peering at her in the gloom.

'Is Holshef here?' Merei asked.

'If you mean that crazy old man, he's downstairs.'

Merei felt some of the tension go out of her shoulders. No one had come to take Holshef away.

'But he can't stay here,' the whiskered alien whined, his dark eyes doleful. 'I haven't been paid. And now that Laxo is—'

'Alternate arrangements are being made,' Merei said, not wanting to revisit the painful subject of how Laxo had met his end. She dug into her bag for credits, remembering how much Laxo had paid to hide people and wincing at the realisation that she had to cover that cost now.

'This is for the week, plus a little for your trouble,' Merei said, handing over the credits. 'You deal only with me – don't tell anyone else that he's here.'

The Lutrillian nodded, and Merei suppressed a smile. Like most thugs, he looked tough but was used to being told what to do.

'Now where is he?' she asked, and the gloomy alien led her to a narrow stairwell almost concealed behind a rusty shipping container.

She found Holshef at the bottom, in a little nest he'd made of ratty pillows and blankets, surrounded by stacks of papers and hard-copy books. Hearing her footsteps on the stairs, the old poet looked up, one pale hand trying to rearrange his halo of wispy white hair.

'Well hello, Miss . . . oh, I'm terribly sorry, I've forgotten your name,' he said.

Merei smiled. 'I never told it to you. Too dangerous, remember?'

'Of course. Such derring-do and intrigue! I suppose from an outsider's point of view it would be rather exciting.'

'I suppose,' Merei said, sitting cross-legged on one of Holshef's scavenged cushions. 'Listen. You'll be here for the next week or so, then we'll move you. I'm not sure where yet.'

'Oh, marvellous!' Holshef said. 'It will be so good to see the sun again, even if it's just for an hour or so. Why, spring must be beginning.'

Merei shook her head, tugging at her jacket. 'It should be, but it's still cold. The dust storms have been terrible.'

'Ah,' Holshef said, his face falling. 'It didn't used to be like this, you know. Spring used to arrive so gently on Lothal – I could tell which week it was by the shade of green in the grasslands and the scent of arrack vine and jogan on the west wind.'

'I love the smell of jogan blossoms,' Merei murmured, remembering the scent that hung over Beck Ollet's orchards when she and Zare had visited.

'When I smell jogan I'm sixteen again,' Holshef said, stroking his upper lip theatrically. 'Tall and strong, with a rakish black moustache. It's the closest thing we poor creatures have to magic, my dear – the ability to be transported through time by a waft of scent that unlocks memory.'

Merei felt her eyes welling up and turned away. Beck had been taken into Imperial custody – she didn't know if he was alive or dead. Zare was in terrible danger, as well. And the orchards had been reduced to bleak pits crawled by mining droids.

'You're sad, my dear,' Holshef said, pressing a little book into her hands. 'Perhaps some poems would help. This volume's all about the fragrances of Lothal in my youth. Before everything changed.'

Merei shoved the little book down into her satchel, feeling her self-control slipping. 'You'll be moved soon,' she said, fleeing for the stairs. 'I promise. Just as soon as I find a safe place.'

As Holshef called out a cheery goodbye, she wondered if safe places still existed on Lothal.

It wasn't the biggest of her worries, not by a long shot, but Merei had found that being a courier for a crime syndicate was a lousy way to keep up your grades. She parked her jumpspeeder and hurried to her first class at Lothal's Vocational School for Institutional Security, mentally sorting through the assignments she had due and vowing that she'd spend the next couple of weeks getting caught up.

But it was impossible to avoid thinking of Holshef and Laxo and everything that had happened. For one thing, the students in her first class included Jix Hekyl, the Pantoran boy who'd arranged her introduction to Laxo's organization and tried to help her erase the account she'd used to break into the Imperial networks. She hadn't seen Jix since warning him not to go to Laxo's headquarters, not long before the stormtroopers had burst in and—

*Don't think about it,* she told herself, aware of Jix's eyes on her. *You didn't know that was going to happen.*

So then why couldn't she meet Jix's gaze?

He caught up with her between classes, grabbing her by the arm when she didn't stop. His face was flushed indigo.

'Glad to see you're all right,' the blue-skinned boy said, but he didn't smile.

'Me too,' she said, coughing and cursing Lothal's persistent dust storms. 'I got lucky. We both did.'

'Some other people weren't so fortunate. What happened, Merei?'

Merei crossed her arms over her chest, watching the other V-SIS students warily.

'An Imperial raid,' she said. 'They didn't get the Grey Syndicate's data, though. I used your pulse-mag to erase everything.'

Jix nodded. 'I figured that, since neither of us is in jail.' He looked around and put his face close to Merei's. 'But I still don't understand why the Empire showed up. Did you tip them off?'

Merei backed away. 'No . . . well, no, not exactly. Things . . . things didn't go the way I wanted them to.'

'I should hope not,' Jix said, angry now. 'People are *dead*, Merei.'

'You think I don't know that?' she demanded, angry now, too. Heads turned in their direction.

'All right,' Jix said. 'I'm sorry. But—'

'But nothing, Jix,' she said, turning away from him. 'We're alive. Alive and free of Laxo. I wish it hadn't happened the way it did, but it's a second chance – and you don't get too many of those. If I were you, I'd make the most of it.'

# CHAPTER 13

**Despite her** vow to focus on her schoolwork, Merei's mind kept returning to the problem of Holshef. She fretted through several classes before finally surrendering to the truth – that there was no safe place for him on Lothal. She had to get him off-world.

At dinner, she waited for an opening in her parents' conversation about the Imperial bureaucracy's latest attempts to make their jobs more difficult, then pounced when she saw one.

'I hear the Empire's cracking down on off-world transport now,' she said to her parents, hoping her voice sounded casual. 'Is that true?'

Her father, Gandr Spanjaf, peered at her with curiosity. 'Planning a vacation, Mer Bear? Do we get to come?'

'That would be awesome, wouldn't it? No, some of

the kids were complaining about it at V-SIS. I wasn't sure what they were talking about.'

'Security has been tightened considerably – that's true,' Jessa Spanjaf told her daughter. 'These days a wildcat launch from the hinterlands will bring a squadron of TIE fighters. But authorised travel is still allowed, of course – subject to an ID check and questioning by security personnel.'

'Questioning? Like what?'

Jessa shrugged. 'Pretty standard stuff. The key isn't the questions themselves but training Imperial officers to spot people who are nervous, or hiding something. Anyone fitting that description gets taken aside for more rigorous questioning.'

Merei tried to imagine Holshef passing such a security check and scowled. The old poet wouldn't stand a chance – and come to think of it, what made her think he'd even be able to memorise the information on a fake ID?

If she was going to get Holshef off-world, it wouldn't be through the spaceport.

Over the next week Merei did better than she'd hoped at focusing on her studies but made no progress in figuring out how to help Holshef. She'd given up on the idea of getting him out through an Imperial facility and didn't want to call on any of Laxo's former associates. She figured most of them would happily sell both her and the poet to bounty hunters.

At the end of the week, she returned to the warehouse on Chapel Street and found the Lutrillian highly agitated and warning about Imperial agents searching for insurgents. Merei managed to get ten more days out of him by paying double the price for a week, but he said that was all he could offer. When Merei tried to argue, he said the poet's hiding space was rented out for a shipment of industrial energy cells coming in from Lantillies. If Holshef wasn't moved by then, he'd be out on the street for whoever cared to claim him.

Merei had trouble sleeping that night. She dreamed she got Holshef a ticket on a secret shuttle launch but arrived at the warehouse to find Yahenna Laxo sitting in the poet's hiding place. The stormtroopers had just arrived when she awoke with a start, whipping her head around in a panic.

There were no stormtroopers in her bedroom – but her datapad was chiming with an incoming comm message.

It was Zare, calling from a comm-house on Arkanis. He seemed to think it was a secure feed, but Merei doubted such a thing existed anymore.

Zare looked exhausted, and she considered not

telling him what she had discovered – that the Inquisitor was behind his transfer to Arkanis. But when she did, Zare didn't look surprised. In fact, he said the Inquisitor had been on Arkanis three days before, and had spoken to him.

Merei looked at him in disbelief, and for a wild moment she imagined he was already in custody and the Imperials had forced him to comm her to establish her own guilt. But then Zare told her he knew where Dhara was being held – and asked her if she could investigate a part of the Academy called Area Null.

There was a terrible hunger in his eyes as he asked, and it frightened her. He would be caught. Suddenly, she was as certain of that as she'd ever been about anything. Zare was smart and brave – it made Merei's heart ache to think of how long he'd lived in fear of being discovered – but he was surrounded by enemies more powerful than he could imagine.

Like Holshef was. Like they all were.

She stammered something about her clearance, scrambling to figure out how she could convince him that he'd be throwing his life away if he persisted in trying to save Dhara. She saw immediately that he didn't understand – that he thought she was afraid for herself. That brought their conversation to a sputtering halt.

'Do you remember the night—' she began, but he'd

been trying to say something at the same time and they'd spoken over each other. When they got it sorted out, she asked if he remembered the smell of jogan blossoms in the Westhills – and she felt a swell of happiness when he said he did. They had lost so much, but if they both remembered that, perhaps they could reclaim some of what had been taken from them.

But then Zare insisted he was close to finding his sister, and Merei found herself pleading with him to run – from the Inquisitor, from the Empire, from everything. He refused to do that, as she'd known he would.

When they said goodbye Merei quickly captured the image of his face on her datapad. She sat staring at it for several minutes, tracing her finger along the contours of his eyes and mouth, pleading with the universe to keep him safe somehow and knowing it wouldn't listen.

# CHAPTER 14

**The next evening** was when everything changed on Lothal. Insurgents seized control of a comm tower and broadcast a message to the planet's people. The message was cut off when the Empire destroyed the tower, disrupting all interplanetary communications. Merei didn't recognise the boy who'd spoken plainly but eloquently about fighting for freedom, but she wondered if he was part of the band she'd helped outside Lothal's Academy, the ones who called themselves the Spectres.

V-SIS was buzzing about the events of the night before, though to Merei's annoyance the students seemed more interested in how the insurgents had sliced into the tower systems than in what they'd actually said. In their first period, their digital-countermeasures instructor informed them that as part of its investigation Imperial Intelligence was reviewing all school records.

'The Empire has been assured that last night's insurgent isn't a V-SIS student,' the instructor said, but then cocked an eyebrow. 'That said, those of you whose extra-curricular activities have been, well, questionable would be wise to cease immediately.'

Merei looked up and found Jix's eyes on her – but then a substantial portion of their class was exchanging looks that were amused, worried, or a bit of both. She started to smile at Jix but then remembered something that left her unable to catch her breath: to throw off Jessa Spanjaf's investigation into the Transportation Ministry data breach, Jix had switched Merei's V-SIS photo with that of a girl in another school. When the Imperials noticed the switch, they might start asking questions . . .

Jix glared at her when she intercepted him in the hall after class, and he only looked angrier when she told him what was worrying her.

'I should have known you needed something – because why else would you talk to me?' he said.

'Jix, that's not fair. I never meant—'

'Forget it. I thought of the photo first thing. I'll switch it in my free period this afternoon.'

She tried to thank him, but he was already marching away.

Dinnertime found both Merei's parents in an uproar. With Lothal's comm tower down, Jessa explained, agencies could access only locally stored information. Data were being fed to courier droids and uploaded to transmitters on orbiting communications ships.

'Which means until we have interplanetary communications restored, every agency is fighting for priority in using courier droids,' Jessa said with a sigh.

'The Empire wouldn't have cut us off from the rest of the galaxy unless there was a real danger,' Gandr said, but Jessa was already shaking her head.

'I think the brass overreacted – they had a tantrum, basically. Now if there's a real threat we'll barely be able to counter it. All security sweeps of the network have been suspended to minimise the system load.'

'What does that mean?' Merei asked.

'A free ride for bad guys,' Jessa growled.

Not so long before, Merei thought with a smile, she would have been appalled to find herself identifying with the bad guys. But things had changed. No sooner had the dishes been cleared than she went to her room and activated her Imperial Security Bureau account. A simple search brought up Holshef's name, along with directives about something called Operation Guiding Light.

Guiding Light, she saw instantly, was an exercise in shaping public opinion about Lothal and its future. Criticism of the Empire was forbidden, of course, but so was anything that focussed on Lothal's past. Nostalgia, the directive said, was a product of dissatisfaction and anger and therefore should be suppressed.

She scanned the list of dissidents and their supposed crimes. They were painters and poets and storytellers – and none of them seemed to have ever so much as picked up a blaster.

Merei downloaded the files and encrypted them on her datapad, smiling when they finished transferring. Then a strange sort of fever came over her and she began systematically downloading everything she had access to – intelligence reports, law-enforcement records, military communications. There was nothing new on Zare and no updates related to Project Harvester. Zare was listed as an active cadet on Arkanis, and Dhara Leonis was marked as suspended.

A look at Beck Ollet's file led Merei to the records about the protests in the Westhills. She read them in horror – bland accounts of 'pacification,' requests that fake departure records be created for protestors who'd been killed, and orders to monitor wives and husbands and children for suspicious activity. And it wasn't just military officers signing off on such cruel and callous measures – Governor Pryce had approved them without the slightest objection.

It was a chilling record of everything that had made Beck determined to fight – even if it cost him his life. They were things Merei had believed couldn't be true.

*I'm so sorry, Beck,* she thought. *For you and for everyone on Lothal. They don't deserve this. Nobody does.*

Finally, she shut down her datapad and got into bed. But sleep didn't come before another thought crept into her mind – and refused to be dislodged.

*Someone has to stop them.*

Merei was one of the first V-SIS students scheduled to meet with the Imperial investigators. She reminded herself to be calm as she walked down the hall to the office the Imperials were using. The Empire had no reason to suspect her of anything, and though she hadn't been able to talk to Jix since their tense discussion in the hallway, she remembered how easy it had been for him to switch her photo. It had probably taken him only a minute or two to switch it back.

The Imperial investigator was in his early twenties and glanced up at her with no apparent interest when she entered the office. He waved for her to sit, then tapped at his datapad and brought her picture up on the office viewscreen.

But the picture wasn't of her – it was of the girl Jix had selected as her replacement.

The young investigator looked at the screen and frowned. Merei sighed and rolled her eyes, praying that the Imperial wouldn't notice that her heart was hammering.

'I keep asking them to fix that,' she said, trying to look indignant. 'I don't even know who that girl is. I mean, how hard can it be to get this right, you know?'

The investigator nodded. 'My access card at headquarters quits working every other day. No one can figure out why. They just tell me to report it to operations.'

They smiled at each other, and Merei answered his questions with what she hoped was the right amount of boredom and mild impatience. When the interview was over, she was exhausted and had to stop in the hallway to calm herself down.

A tall, blue-skinned figure was hurrying her way.

'Jix,' she breathed. 'I thought you were going to switch the photos!'

'I tried! They'd locked down the system!'

'So why didn't you tell me?'

Jix looked at his feet. 'I don't know. I just . . . I didn't want to let you down.'

'Let me down?' Her laughter was a humourless bark. 'I almost wet my pants in there! That probably would have seemed suspicious, don't you think?'

'I'm sorry, Merei,' Jix said miserably. 'I really am.'

'Forget it – no harm was done,' she said. 'But you better get yourself together before your own interview.'

Jix nodded and slunk away.

*Poor boy. He just isn't cut out for the criminal life,* she thought, then smiled ruefully. *Though apparently I am.*

Merei let out a long breath. She hadn't been that scared since the first time she'd lined up to attempt a game-winning kick in grav-ball, years before on Corulag.

*I made that kick, though,* she thought, then brightened. Remembering grav-ball had given her an idea.

It was a long ride out to the dingy watering hole run by the grizzled Ithorian known as Old Jho. Merei had always protested when Laxo sent her out there with the pirated grav-ball holos that Old Jho loved and was willing to pay a premium for.

She eyed the Pit Stop warily, shaking the dust out of the face mask she'd worn on the journey, but there wasn't so much as a speeder bike outside. Old Jho himself was sitting behind the counter in the empty cantina, watching a holo that he hurriedly switched off when she walked through the doors.

'It's you,' he grunted, the bubbling Ithorian language turned into electronically modulated Basic by a translator around his neck. 'I've had to look for another source of holos, you know.'

'I know – sorry about that.'

Old Jho shrugged. 'Drink?'

'I'm only fifteen,' Merei said, faintly shocked.

'That's right. Forgot you were such a strong supporter of law and order on Lothal.'

'Very funny. I'll take an ice water,' Merei said. 'Look, I came here on my own business.'

Old Jho handed over the water and eyed her grumpily.

'I have a friend who needs a ticket off Lothal,' she said. 'One that won't require proper ID.'

'Not easy to do these days – what with the blockade and all the trouble.'

'Even if it's life or death?'

Old Jho waved his long fingers dismissively. They sat in silence for a moment, the only sound the clunk of ice cubes in Merei's tumbler of water.

'So what did Laxo owe your friend?' the bartender asked.

'Nothing. He was hiding him from the Empire. Now there's no one left to do it.'

'Bright young kid like you ought to be glad to be free of bad influences like Laxo,' Old Jho muttered. 'Instead, here you are looking for more trouble.'

'I know,' Merei said. 'It's just this last bit of business I need to clear up.'

Old Jho leaned his skinny brown forearms on the bar. 'That's always the bit of business that puts you in prison, young one. What did this friend of yours do to anger the Empire, anyway?'

'Wrote poetry.'

The Ithorian squinted at her, cocking his head in confusion.

'Here,' Merei said, digging in her satchel for Holshef's book of poems.

Old Jho retrieved a pair of monocles from beneath the bar, fitting each one over a dark beady eye. He read in silence, nothing moving except his eyes and the fingertip that turned each page. Then he set the book down and looked at it in silence.

'I like the one about the spine trees of Pelamir Gorge,' Old Jho said after a moment. 'I went there often as a juvenile. I remember the sound the wind made in the tree cones and the taste of the root tea. And the crisp smell of the needles in winter. The forests are all cut down now. Turned into mines and machines.'

Merei just waited.

'You have credits?' the Ithorian asked, then grunted when Merei nodded. 'People owe me a favour. People with a ship. They're lying low right now, but I can get a message to them. Bring your friend here in six days.'

# CHAPTER 15

**When Merei** visited Holshef four days later, she was prepared for any number of problems – the Lutrillian shaking her down for more credits, lurking bounty hunters, even an Imperial raid.

It hadn't occurred to her that Holshef might refuse to leave.

'Leave Lothal?' he asked. 'Oh, no, my dear. You're very kind, but this is my home – the only home I've ever known. My grandmother came here as a young woman. She built our house – Capital City's grown up around it, but it's still our house. My people are buried here. My memories are here. What you ask is impossible.'

'I've spoken to your daughter – the one on Eriadu,' Merei said. 'The temporary communications link they've set up is terrible, but we were able to talk. She'll be on Garel the day after tomorrow to meet you.'

'Impossible,' Holshef said. 'Living the rest of my life

without the sound of the wind in the grasslands? Or the sight of thunderheads rolling in over the mountains?'

'Holshef, you have to listen to me. If you stay here you'll never see or hear those things again. They'll put you in a cell and all you'll see is metal. And all you'll hear is machines.'

'For the time being. But someday it will be different.'

Merei got up and began to pace, agitated. 'You don't have a lot of somedays left!'

'Which is all the more reason to spend the few I have here. On my home planet. Oh, I don't blame you for not understanding, dear – you're not from here.'

'But I *do* understand,' Merei said. 'I came here from Corulag – it's a city world, mostly ruined. I hadn't been here very long when friends took me to the jogan orchards in the Westhills. My friend . . . he said on a warm autumn night that was the sweetest-smelling place in the whole galaxy.'

Holshef stared off into the distance. 'He might have been right.'

'That place – it's gone,' Merei said. 'The Empire turned it into a mine and killed the people who dared to protest. Then it told their families they'd gone off-world. There have been dust storms all winter. People have started wearing face masks so they don't walk around coughing and spitting dirt. Half the nights you can't see the stars. The home you love no longer exists, Holshef – it's being dismantled and destroyed even as we speak. And the Empire isn't going to stop until there's nothing left.'

'Which is why people have to know,' Holshef said. 'They have to understand what's been lost.'

'I agree,' Merei said. 'But it's too late to tell the people of Lothal – they already know. You have to tell the rest of the galaxy. And you can't do that here.'

Holshef looked down at his hands, twisting them back and forth in his lap.

'You've never told me your name,' he said softly.

'It's Merei Spanjaf.'

'All right, Merei Spanjaf – I'll go,' Holshef said, so quietly Merei barely heard him. Then he bowed his head and began to weep.

Merei arrived at V-SIS a few minutes before her first class, coated with dust but pleased that Holshef had agreed to her plan. If she could just get through the day, she would take him to Old Jho in the morning, where his ride to Garel should be waiting.

She saw Jix in the hallway and yelled to him, waving when he turned. Jix looked more at ease, too, she noticed. That was also good news. Class was difficult enough without finding herself on the other end of reproachful stares and haunted looks.

'How was your interview?' she asked him, remembering that it had been scheduled for the previous afternoon.

'Fine,' Jix said. 'The interviewer was actually a nice guy for an Imperial. He asked me a bunch of questions about repeater services and info-houses, but it was all pretty casual.'

'They asked you about *what*?' Merei asked.

'Repeater services and info-houses. You mean they didn't ask you about that stuff?'

'No, Jix. They didn't ask me about any of that.'

The class bell rang, and they went their separate ways. A voice in Merei's head was screaming for her to run, right now. But she couldn't do that – not yet, not when she was so close to getting Holshef to safety.

She and Jix had the first class after lunch together. Merei was relieved to see the Pantoran boy in his usual seat in the front row. She'd half-suspected that he wouldn't be there and she'd hear he'd been arrested. She finally let herself relax when class began, with their instructor asking them about the first principles of security.

The doors at the back of the classroom opened and Merei braced for her teacher to give whoever was late a savage dressing-down. But then the teacher's eyes widened and he took a couple of steps backward.

She turned and saw an Imperial officer walking down the aisle, followed by two stormtroopers. The officer's eyes turned from side to side, surveying the muttering students.

'Jix Hekyl?' he snapped.

Jix got unsteadily to his feet, his cheeks white. The stormtroopers cuffed his wrists behind his back and indicated that he was to precede them out of the classroom. Merei stared at them, heart hammering, waiting for her name to be called.

The trio of Imperials exited the room in silence.

The rest of the class passed in a blur. When it was finally over, Merei shoved through the students and raced to one of the computer labs downstairs. She checked that her transmissions were encrypted and tapped into the Imperial network.

She found the warrant for Jix's arrest, but there was no other information. She looked at the list of warrants. Her own name wasn't there, but one name stopped her.

*Hestia Tarleton. Who's Hestia Tarleton?*

Then she remembered and felt like she'd been punched in the stomach. Hestia Tarleton was the girl whose photo Jix had swapped with Merei's – the one he'd failed to switch back. She was a student at some seminary on the far side of Capital City.

*The Empire must have picked her up instead of me.*

That meant Merei had hours at most.

# CHAPTER 16

**Jessa Spanjaf** was not pleased.

'Merei? Are you comming me while you're riding your jumpspeeder? You know how unsafe that is. And why does your voice sound strange?'

'Because it's encrypted, Mother,' Merei yelled over the wind and traffic as she cut between a droid truck and a fancy civilian speeder. 'I need you to encrypt your end and comm me back from somewhere private. And I need you to do it right now.'

'What in the world is this about?'

'Just do it, Mother.'

Thirty seconds later Jessa was back, her own voice tinny and distorted.

'This had better be good,' she said.

'I don't have time to explain,' Merei said. 'You and Dad need to get out of Capital City right now. I'll send the coordinates – it's beyond the Easthills. Don't tell anybody, and don't go to the apartment. It isn't safe.'

Jessa was silent long enough that Merei worried the connection had been lost.

'Is this some kind of joke?' she asked finally.

'I wish.'

'Are you in trouble?'

'We all are. Go to the coordinates I send you. I'll be there as soon as I can. I have something I need to do first.'

Strangely, Merei felt better than she had in weeks. There was no more reason to look over her shoulder or worry about what might happen. Now all she could do was act.

She raced across Capital City and pulled up in front of Holshef's warehouse hideaway. When she went downstairs, the old poet smiled at her and started to heat water on his portable stove, but Merei cut him off with an upraised hand.

'We're leaving – right now,' she said.

'Today's youth are always in a hurry,' Holshef said, but obediently began to consolidate several tall stacks of papers.

Merei gaped at him. 'What are you doing? We need to go. And we're not taking anything.'

'But my poems!'

'Poetry isn't going to save us, Holshef.'

'Not even my latest ones?' he asked plaintively. Merei knew that tone – he'd wheedle with her for hours until she gave in.

'All right, but just the latest ones.'

Merei watched with mounting agitation as Holshef sorted a tall stack of paper into a marginally less tall stack of paper.

'Just the *latest* poems,' she said.

'I heard you, my dear. These are the poems I composed during the last year.'

Merei closed her eyes, trying to remain calm. 'You can take the last week's.'

Under Merei's direction the old poet gathered a much smaller stack of paper and stuffed it into a threadbare messenger bag that he slung over his shoulder. She led him upstairs, saluted the nervous Lutrillian, and looked in both directions down the street before sitting astride her bike. Holshef blinked at the sunshine and smiled, then shakily got on the jumpspeeder behind her.

'You have to hold on more tightly,' she told him.

'But you are a delicate child – my grip will harm you. And I don't want to jumble my papers.'

'Falling off the bike will do a lot worse than that,' Merei said, pressing the accelerator slightly harder.

Even that gentle bit of acceleration left Holshef waving his hands frantically.

'My word!' he exclaimed. 'I didn't spend my youth in a swoop gang, you know. I spent it at the reliquary of Saint—'

*'Listen to me,'* Merei said. 'We're in danger. We're going to go as fast as we can without getting stopped by a patrol. And if a patrol does try to stop us, we're going to have to go a lot faster than that. So I need you to do two things. First, *shut up*. Second, hold on tighter than you've ever held on before.'

That shocked the old poet into silence. He nodded, shifted his bag to one side, and squeezed Merei around her stomach. When she was satisfied that he wasn't going to fall off, she gunned the jumpspeeder and streaked down Chapel Street.

They passed through the outskirts of Capital City without incident and reached the highway leading through the grasslands to the east of the city. It was mid-afternoon, but traffic was already heavy. The highway was filled with civilian speeders whose drivers were headed out of town for the weekend, along with aged farm vehicles and droid trucks. Merei was careful to stay below the posted speed limit, but the handful of Imperial patrol vehicles they saw took no notice of them. Merei glanced at her jumpspeeder's nav unit and saw they were just a couple of klicks from Old Jho's.

*We're going to make it,* she thought to herself in amazement.

That was when a blaster bolt nearly took her head off.

Heart thudding in her chest, Merei cut left, nearly clipping a farm truck. The jumpspeeder fishtailed and Holshef grabbed frantically at Merei, pulling her hair painfully but somehow managing not to fall off. She stomped on the accelerator, cutting between a pair of speeder tankers, and risked a glance over her shoulder.

It wasn't the Imperials chasing them but a swoop, some kind of sport model. Merei tried to look at the rider, but they were going too fast and she got only an impression of a black-clad figure holding a chrome blaster that glinted in the sun.

'His ride's a lot faster than mine,' Merei said. 'Hang on!'

'I *am* hanging on!' Holshef wailed.

'Then hang on harder!'

She dodged in front of a speeder truck, slowed down, and lurched her jumpspeeder back and forth. A flesh-and-blood driver behind her might have panicked, but she knew the vehicle's droid brain would adjust automatically and placidly to her manoeuvres, ideally stalling their pursuer. It had been a favourite game of bored teenage swoop jockeys on Corulag.

The speeder truck honked at Merei, which she ignored. She risked another look backward but couldn't see the swoop. Then she caught a glimpse of it to their left. The rider had gunned his engine in an effort to escape the snarled traffic and flank them. He fired, the blasts gouging craters in the roadway as Merei cut to the right to let the speeder truck pass.

'That maniac is going to get someone hurt!' Holshef shouted.

She accelerated alongside a double tanker truck, trying to think along with their pursuer and simultaneously look for something – anything – that she could use against him. But it was all she could do to keep from crashing, and every five seconds she had to remind Holshef to hold on.

A blaster bolt grazed her jumpspeeder's control yoke, sending up sparks. Their pursuer had managed to get behind them. Merei tried desperately to cut to the left, but a flurry of blaster bolts dissuaded her. Whoever was chasing them wasn't trying to kill them – from that angle he could have done so easily enough – but to drive them off the road.

*It's the hunter who's been after Holshef,* she realised. *He wants his bounty.*

Holshef shifted on the jumpspeeder behind Merei, trying to steal a glance at their pursuer. His left hand came free and she felt his grip on her middle slipping. She screamed at him to hold on, the jumpspeeder weaving drunkenly. Horns blared all around them.

'My papers!' Holshef yelled.

Merei looked back and saw Holshef clinging desperately to his bag, which had slipped off his shoulder and was now pointed straight out behind them. She screamed for him to let go before the wind dragged him off the bike after it, but he either didn't hear her or wouldn't listen. The bag opened and papers began streaming out of it, a tide of white that stuck to windshields and air intakes behind them.

One of the pieces of paper hit the swoop rider in the face and stuck there, pinned by the wind.

The bounty hunter pawed desperately at the paper obscuring his vision. His swoop wobbled and he grabbed at the control yoke, overcompensating. The swoop tumbled out of control and vanished between two fuel tanks being hauled by a droid truck. The tanker truck lurched sickeningly to the left, headlights flashing a warning to other drivers.

'Holshef! Let go of the bag!' Merei screamed, stomping on the accelerator. A moment later she felt heat on her back and an enormous explosion shoved at the bike.

When she looked back, the tanker truck was a burning shell and scraps of flaming paper were drifting through the air.

'Let that be a lesson for you, my dear,' Holshef said. 'Never underestimate the power of poetry.'

# CHAPTER 17

**To Merei's relief,** Jessa and Gandr were sitting at the bar in Old Jho's Pit Stop. But she could tell the Ithorian bartender was furious even before he began yelling at her that she was a day early and on top of that how dare she bring Imperial Intelligence types to his place. The diatribe was so impassioned and rapid-fire that his translator couldn't keep up and lapsed into silence. Then her mother was yelling at her, too, while Holshef tried to tell everyone about their thrilling escape.

'There was an arrest warrant out for me,' Merei said when Old Jho finally paused for breath. 'Well, not exactly for me but close enough. I had to move. As for these Imperial Intelligence types, they're my parents. And *this* is Holshef – you've read his poetry.'

The Ithorian paused and glanced at the old poet.

'Your reminiscence of the Westhills harvest was

fine work,' Old Jho said. 'Did you ever taste greel-wood syrup from Far Hiradne?'

Holshef smiled. 'My first job was as an apprentice sap collector there.'

'I have a bottle of vintage Hiradne syrup in the back,' Old Jho said, and a moment later the Ithorian and the human poet were trundling that way, trading recollections of bygone days on Lothal.

Merei turned to her parents. Jessa looked too enraged to form speech.

'I think you'd better tell us what this is all about, Mer Bear,' Gandr said quietly.

'I know,' Merei said, and took a deep breath. 'So remember that break-in at the Transportation Ministry? The one Mum was investigating? Um, that was me. I left thumb drives in the ministry that contained a snooper program created by the Grey Syndicate. When someone installed them I was able to get admin privileges on the Imperial network, and I used the admin account to create a fake ISB identity that let me steal Imperial documents for Zare. The snooper would have erased itself except for the one terminal that had a bad chronometer, but you knew that part. Oh, and then the Grey Syndicate's boss forced me to keep working for him as a courier. I got out of that by kidnapping myself and erased their records with a pulse-mag. But the Empire arrested a V-SIS student who helped me and I knew he'd never be able to resist interrogation, and they've already arrested the girl they think is me, so we need to get off-planet as quickly as possible. And get new identities if we want to stay out of prison, I suppose, but first things first.'

Her parents just looked at her for a long moment.

'Wow,' her father said. 'That's some impressive slicing, Mer Bear. Thumb drives, huh? Did the snooper use a—'

'Gandr!' Jessa said sharply. 'I hardly think that's the most important thing we have to discuss right now.'

'Right. Right. Of course. Mer Bear, this is really disappointing—'

'Do you realise what you've done?' Jessa demanded. 'You've ruined all our lives. You've become some kind of insurgent – an enemy of the Empire that's employed us and allowed us to make a living and—'

'Mother, stop,' Merei said, extracting her datapad from her satchel. 'I downloaded a lot of documents from the Imperial network about what's been happening on Lothal in recent months. Before you say anything else, I want you to read them. Read them, and then we'll talk.'

Jessa looked at the datapad almost unwillingly, then shrugged and took it from her daughter.

'Our ride to Garel doesn't get here until tomorrow

morning, so you have plenty of time,' Merei said. 'Well, unless the stormtroopers get here first.'

Jessa tapped at the datapad's screen and eyed the list of files, then peered at Merei.

'Most of these documents are highly classified,' she said.

'I know they are,' Merei said. 'My clearance is a lot higher than yours, Mum.'

Jessa and Gandr took Merei's datapad down into a storeroom beneath Old Jho's, leaving Merei to slump down on her arms at the bar, the events of the day finally catching up with her. She sat there quietly after Holshef and Old Jho returned, chattering away about vanished wonders of Lothal, and sat up only when Jessa reappeared, her face pale.

Her mother settled in the seat beside Merei, staring down at the bar.

'I didn't know,' she said quietly. 'I suspected things were happening, maybe. But I didn't know.'

'None of us did,' Merei said.

'But you've taken some awful chances, Merei,' Jessa said. 'The way you broke in and created your identity – you've left trails all over the place for someone to follow, if they know what they're looking for.'

'I couldn't exactly ask you for help.'

'I suppose that's true.'

'So what happens now?' Merei asked.

'That will depend on whether the Empire thinks your classmate is connected to something more than low-level slicing for some two-credit operation,' Jessa said.

'Jix,' Merei said. 'What will happen to him?'

Jessa shook her head. 'He's beyond our help. Just hope he draws a short sentence. But once the Empire figures out it's looking for you, our faces will be in the memory of every probe droid on Lothal. And it'll start investigating your associates. By then, hopefully, we'll be safe on Garel. Your father's already transferring our credits to places the Empire will have trouble freezing them.'

Merei nodded, surprised and impressed by her mother's level-headed acceptance of what had happened.

'What about Zare?' Merei asked. 'He has enough problems without my endangering him. But I can check his status—'

'There's no point – not with him on Arkanis,' Jessa said. 'Records like that aren't updating in real time yet. We'll have to look in the morning, when the courier droids have done their work.'

Merei didn't think she'd be able to sleep, particularly not crammed into Old Jho's storeroom with her parents and Holshef. But she did – so soundly that when she woke up her chronometer said it was nearly two hours after dawn. She looked around, alarmed, and found her parents hunched over their datapads, eating ration bars.

'Where's Holshef?' Merei asked.

'Mooning over wildflowers with your friend Jho,' Gandr said with a smile.

'Since you're finally up, let's get down to business,' Jessa said. 'There's no warrant for your arrest yet, but there *is* an inquiry into the accident on the highway – and Hestia Tarleton was released last night.'

'That's one thing off my conscience, at least,' Merei said. 'But what about Zare? Have the courier droids completed their updates?'

'The morning updates are still loading,' Jessa said. 'In the meantime, I've been using your ISB clearance to see what I can find out about Area Null. It looks like the Empire runs a number of secret programs out of there. Are any of these names familiar?'

Jessa held out Merei's datapad. Merei took it and scanned the list.

'Project Harvester is the reason the Empire

kidnapped Zare's sister, Dhara,' Merei said. 'I don't recognise these others, but . . . oh, no.'

'What is it?'

'Project Unity. That's the program they put our friend Beck Ollet in. From AppSci, remember? It's a re-education program for former dissidents. If Beck's in Area Null and Zare tries to get in there . . .'

Jessa nodded grimly.

'Let's not overreact until we see the updates,' she said. 'Why don't you go upstairs and see what's happening with our ride to Garel? If there's any news I'll come find you.'

Merei started to protest, but realised her mother was right. It would do her no good to fidget while her datapad loaded information.

When she emerged from the storeroom, she was surprised to see Jho back at the bar, speaking to a hologram. Holshef was sitting at a table, scribbling with a stylus.

Old Jho waved her over to stand beside him in front of the holoprojector. She recognised the shimmering image as the hulking Lasat she knew only as Spectre-4.

'Well, if it ain't Merei-1,' he said, grinning. 'Always figured you'd come to a bad end.'

'Are you our ride?' Merei asked.

The Lasat's ears drooped and he looked away.

'Yeah, about that,' he said. 'Like I told Jho, Lothal's a mite too hot for me and my associates at the moment – half the Empire's looking for us on account of a few noses we bloodied. But don't worry, Merei-1 – we'll meet you at the edge of the Garel system. Jho's going to run you out to us in that old crate of his, and from there we'll take you to Garel.'

'Which means your crew still owes me that favour,' Old Jho grumbled, cutting off the transmission and shaking his head.

'I didn't know you had a ship,' Merei said as the Ithorian extracted a battered toolbox from beneath the bar.

Old Jho nodded. 'Hyperdrive's motivator's a mite iffy, but should hold up for such a short trip. It'll fly. Well, after I fix a few things.'

'A few things?' Merei asked, not liking the sound of that. 'Where is this ship of yours, anyway? I didn't see it coming in.'

'Behind the Pit Stop, under a tarp.'

'Oh, boy. When's the last time it was in space?'

'A while ago,' Old Jho said, quizzically comparing a pair of Harris wrenches. 'Like all sensible beings, I prefer to stay on the ground. Plus I get spacesick.'

Jessa emerged from the storeroom, with Gandr behind her. From her mother's expression Merei knew instantly that it was bad news.

'Zare's cadet status is suspended,' she said. 'He's been arrested and is scheduled for a military tribunal.'

'Oh, no!'

Merei turned to Old Jho, who was rummaging through his toolbox at a glacial pace.

'We have to go! Right now!'

'The ship's not ready to fly.'

'It has to be! We need—'

'Merei,' Jessa said. 'You need to calm down.'

'Don't tell me to calm down! They've caught Zare and they're going to kill him! And it's all my fault!'

'It doesn't have anything to do with you,' Jessa said. 'The Empire hasn't realised it's looking for you yet, remember? This is something else.'

That was true. Merei forced herself to breathe, to think.

'The Empire will arrest Zare's parents,' she said.

'Yes,' Jessa said.

'So we have to help them.'

'Whoa, Mer Bear,' Gandr said. 'Capital City's not exactly over the next hill. We have to get off this planet as quickly as possible.'

'Not without Tepha and Leo,' Merei said, crossing her arms over her chest. 'Jho, how long before we're ready to fly?'

The Ithorian shrugged. 'A couple of hours.'

'That's how long we need to get to Capital City anyway,' Merei said, turning to her mother.

Jessa sighed. 'I'm going to regret this. We'll take our speeder – unless you can figure out how to get three people on a jumpspeeder.'

Gandr paled. 'Jess, that's insane.'

'This whole thing's insane,' Jessa said. 'Fortunately, we forged our speeder's transponder code last night in case we had to make a run for it. Merei, do you still have your locator?'

Merei nodded, digging in her bag for the device her father had given her – the one that had led the stormtroopers to the Grey Syndicate's headquarters.

'Leave it with your father,' Jessa said. 'We'll get Zare's parents out, head west from Capital City, and send you our location.'

'And if the ship's not ready to fly by then?' Gandr asked.

'Then we'll improvise,' Jessa said.

As Merei turned to follow her mother, long fingers gripped her arm. Old Jho handed her an antique blaster pistol.

'That's not exactly my specialty,' Merei said doubtfully.

'It is a barbaric way of solving a problem,' Old Jho said. 'But it can also be an effective one.'

# CHAPTER 18

**Merei expected** her mother to object to the blaster, but Jessa just glanced at it and told her to keep the safety on. Merei wanted to laugh. A day before the conversation would have been inconceivable, but now everything about their lives was inconceivable.

As the Spanjafs' speeder neared Capital City, Merei felt her stomach twisting. The mushroom-shaped Imperial headquarters and the white bulk of the Academy seemed filled with peril, and she expected troop transports and gunships to appear at any moment. But it was a day like any other on Lothal. Jessa even got a parking place just a few metres from the Leonises' apartment.

Merei scanned the street, but nothing seemed out of the ordinary. She got out of the vehicle, painfully aware of the blaster in her bag, and pressed the Leonises' call button.

*This would be a really lousy time to be out doing errands, Tepha,* she thought.

'Leonis residence,' Auntie Nags said in her usual prim tone. 'Please state your business.'

'It's Merei Spanjaf, Nags. Please tell Tepha it's urgent.'

Tepha met them at the front door, looking alarmed. Leo Leonis was walking toward them, smiling politely.

'Tepha, no time to explain – we have to go right now. My mother has a speeder downstairs.'

'Young lady, what can you be talking about?' demanded Nags, photoreceptors flaring red. Behind her, the smile disappeared from Leo Leonis's face.

'Be quiet, Nags,' Tepha said, her face turning grey with fear. 'It's Zare, isn't it? What's happened?'

'Zare?' Leo asked. 'What's this about Zare?'

'He's been arrested on Arkanis and is scheduled for interrogation and a military tribunal,' Merei said. 'Which means they'll find out everything – and even before they do, they'll come here and take you into custody.'

Tepha's hand flew to her mouth. Nags began to pace in a circle, her servomotors whining. Leo gaped at Merei.

'Arrested?' he managed at last. 'Is this some kind of joke? Arrested for what?'

'Leo, we have to go,' Tepha said, and Merei was relieved to hear her voice was firm.

'We're not going anywhere until I know what this is about,' Leo said.

Merei took a deep breath.

'The Empire kidnapped Dhara as part of something called Project Harvester,' Merei said. 'No, Mr. Leonis, don't interrupt me. You need to hear this. Zare entered the Academy to try to find her, while using his cadet clearance to feed secret Imperial information to the insurgents here on Lothal. He discovered Dhara's being held prisoner on Arkanis. But something must have gone wrong, because now he's in Imperial custody, too.'

'You're delusional,' Leo said, hands balling into fists. 'These are *lies*. Our son would never do such things. And the Empire is doing everything it can to find Dhara and bring her back to us.'

'I can prove to you that isn't true,' Merei began, hunting for her datapad and finding Old Jho's antique pistol instead. She shoved it aside and dug deeper.

'If you won't listen to her, listen to *me*,' Tepha urged her husband. 'All of this is true. I've known it since Zare discovered what happened to Dhara and told me his plan.'

*'And you didn't tell me?'* Leo screamed.

'No. Because I knew you'd react like this.'

Leo just stared at his wife. His mouth moved, but no sound came out.

'You've all gone crazy,' he said finally.

'Leo, if you want to wait for the Empire to manufacture some lie about how our son died, go ahead,' Tepha said. 'But you'll be doing it alone.'

Merei thrust the datapad at Leo. 'It's all here, Mr. Leonis – Dhara's file and Zare's, too. See for yourself.'

Leo shoved the datapad away. 'I'm not looking at your fake documents. There's been some kind of misunderstanding. I'm contacting the authorities to straighten it out.'

He'd taken two steps when Merei shot him, the blue concentric stun beams catching him in the back. He staggered and flopped onto the couch. Auntie Nags turned to Merei, photoreceptors brilliant red.

'Before you say anything, Nags, I wish I'd done that months ago,' Tepha said. 'Now let's get Leo down to the speeder.'

They were on the western fringes of Capital City when Leo began to wake up, lifting his head woozily from Auntie Nags's synthflesh shoulder.

'Merei, we've got your locator,' Gandr said over Merei's comlink. 'We'll pick you up a few kilometres out of town. There's a farm road off the highway where we can land. If Jho's ship doesn't fall out of the sky first.'

'Got it – see you soon,' Merei said. 'Mum, can't you go any faster?'

'This isn't exactly the time to get stopped for speeding,' Jessa said, her eyes scanning the streets around them.

The warehouses gave way to single-storey adobe buildings, then a patchwork of homes and empty fields, and then they were surrounded by the grasslands of Lothal, with Capital City behind them.

'We're just a couple of klicks away,' Merei said. 'But I don't see the ship yet.'

Ahead of them the highway curved, and Merei remembered riding that way to the Barchetta River and the Westhills beyond it. She looked off to their right, hoping to catch a glimpse of the hills where so much had been set in motion.

Then Jessa slammed on the brakes. Tepha gasped and Merei braced herself.

'Mum, what—'

'Speeder bikes,' Jessa said. 'It's a roadblock.'

Merei saw them now – two bikes, positioned across the highway. Their drivers were standing in the road, one hand up to halt them.

'There was an intersection a few hundred metres back,' Merei said. 'Hurry!'

'Behind us!' Tepha cried out, and Merei saw two more speeder bikes coming up fast from the direction of Capital City.

'It's over,' Jessa said. 'We tried.'

'Oh, dear, oh, dear,' said Nags.

'It's *not* over,' Merei said, pulling the blaster out of her satchel. But her mother grabbed her wrist, eyes blazing.

'I'm afraid it is,' Jessa said. 'Put the gun away, Merei. Things are bad enough.'

The bikes glided to a halt behind them, and their drivers began barking orders. Merei and Jessa stepped out of the speeder with their hands above their heads, followed by Tepha and Auntie Nags. One of the Imperials walked toward them, blaster raised. Tepha was trying to explain about Leo in the backseat.

'We were so close,' Merei muttered.

And then the world was full of heat, light, and noise. The bikes were reduced to burning wreckage, and the two Imperials lay sprawled on the roadway.

A boxy freight hauler roared overhead, its engines whining and coughing. A turret on its underside turned jerkily forward and spat fire, sending the other two bikes and their drivers flying. The ship banked awkwardly to port and headed back toward them, slowing and firing manoeuvring jets.

'Come on!' Merei yelled to the others as Jho's freight hauler settled onto the roadway, its ramp already descending to receive them.

# PART 3:
# THE TOWER

# CHAPTER 19

**It struck** Zare as bitterly funny that they made him wear his dress uniform for the tribunal.

Habit made him put it on carefully, checking that his boots were properly shined and his ceremonial sabre hung from his belt at the approved angle. That struck him as even funnier, in an equally bitter way.

*What will they do if my shirt's untucked? Shoot me?*

When Pocarto nodded at him, Zare didn't hesitate but strode into the ceremonial chamber within Area Null, the one he'd never reached. He smiled at the clatter of the stormtroopers' armour behind him as they hurried to catch up.

Colonel Julyan was sitting in a carved wooden chair on a dais at the far end of the room. In front of him, on a bench, sat the eleven other Commandant's Cadets, also in their dress uniforms. A small knot of Imperial officers sat below the windows. Among them was Commandant Hux, with DeeDee at his side. Zare studied them in turn, only dropping his eyes when he came to the pale, miserable face of Chiron.

Julyan rapped his gavel on the desk in front of him and waved Zare to a solitary seat in the middle of the room. Zare adjusted his sabre and settled into the chair, conscious of the stormtroopers behind him. He heard the waves outside, beating against the foundations of the tower, and smelled the tang of the sea.

Zare wondered if they would go over the evidence against him yet again, rehashing what they'd learned from questioning Beck and what Zare had confirmed under interrogation.

He'd told them everything he knew about Dev Morgan, grimly pleased by the certainty that none of it would be of use to them. The only thing he hadn't revealed, during those hours the interrogation droid had hovered above him, was the nature of Chiron's mission on Arkanis. But there was no heroism in that – if his interrogators had asked, he would have told them about it. He would have done anything to make the hovering black droid stop what it was doing to him.

Zare braced himself for a lengthy review of all he'd done, but Julyan seemed determined to run the tribunal as briskly as one of his classroom discussions.

'Rise, Cadet Leonis,' Julyan said. 'You are charged

with fraudulent enlistment, making false official statements, perjuring your oath as a cadet, refusal to obey lawful orders, conduct unbecoming a cadet, dereliction of duty, destruction of Imperial property, conspiracy, providing aid and comfort to the enemies of the Galactic Empire, espionage, assault on Imperial personnel, attempted murder of Imperial personnel, sedition, and treason. You have reviewed the evidence against you. How do you plead?'

'Guilty on all counts,' Zare said, relieved to hear his voice was firm and clear.

'I see. And do you have anything to say in your defence?'

Zare scanned the cold faces of the Commandant's Cadets – Anya Razar, Orman le Hivre, Rav Horan, and the others. His eyes passed over Hux, moved to Pocarto, and finally settled on the stricken Chiron.

'I do,' he said. 'All I ever wanted was to be a servant of the Empire – to make the galaxy a better place. But then I saw the Empire for what it really was. The Empire made me learn lies at school. One of its lowliest officials wouldn't let my grav-ball teammates play because they were the wrong species. It ruined my adopted homeworld because that was cheaper and easier than doing the right thing. It trained me to use the law not for keeping order but for spreading fear. It murdered people for no crime except wanting it to live up to its own propaganda.'

He scanned the faces in the chamber, looking for some sign that his words were connecting with somebody – anybody.

'And the Empire kidnapped my sister – kidnapped her and lied about it to my parents,' he said. 'My sister, who wanted to serve the Empire even more than I did. I saw all these things, and I knew I couldn't be silent. I knew I had to resist. To stop these things from happening. Or at least to try.'

He swallowed, his mouth dry. 'And every day, on every planet in the Empire, more people are realising what I've realised and saying what I've said and doing what I've done. I'm going to be silenced. I'm going to be killed. I know that. But the Empire can't silence all the people like me. It can't kill all the people like me. Or it will be an Empire that rules nothing. That *is* nothing.'

For a moment there was no sound but the waves' slapping at the foundations of the tower.

'Is that all, cadet?' Julyan asked.

Zare simply nodded.

'All rise,' Julyan said. 'First, Cadet Leonis, you are expelled from Imperial service. Your fellow cadets shall administer the sentence.'

The Commandant's Cadets stepped forward. Zare

stood in silence as they surrounded him, as their hands went to his uniform. He was tugged this way and that, and then the ceremonial braid parted from the fabric on his shoulder, followed by buttons popping and cloth tearing. They ripped the dress uniform from his body, leaving him in a T-shirt and knee-length shorts.

Le Hivre had Zare's ceremonial sabre. He drew it from its scabbard, staring coldly at Zare, then broke it over his knee. The pieces of the discarded weapon rang on the floor. The cadets turned their backs to him, forming a line.

Julyan eyed him. 'Second, Zare Leonis, you are sentenced to death for crimes against the Empire. The sentence shall be carried out in the morning, by firing squad. Return the prisoner to his cell.'

Night came to Arkanis. Zare stood on the bunk in his cell, peering through a narrow window in the ancient stone. He heard the rain beating on the glass and the crash of the waves far below.

The door to the cell slid aside. Chiron entered, nodding to the stormtroopers outside, then sat down on the bench opposite Zare's bunk.

'Why didn't you tell me?' Chiron asked, his voice low and pained. 'I did everything I could to help you, Zare. I tried to find your sister. You know I did.'

Zare turned back to the window. 'If I had, what would you have done?'

'I would have gone to the sector governor,' Chiron said. 'Or to Grand Moff Tarkin. Or to Coruscant. What happened to your sister is terrible. The things you spoke of today are terrible. But they're abuses committed by a misguided few – perversions of Imperial policy.'

Zare shook his head.

'I wish that were true,' he said. 'But *you're* the misguided one. If I'd told you, you would have tried to help me. I believe that. But then I would have disappeared, too. The Empire you believe in is an illusion, Lieutenant Chiron – a *lie*. The real Empire is the Empire of Athletic Director Fhurek and Captain Roddance and the Inquisitor. And Tarkin and Palpatine.'

Chiron said nothing for a moment, turning his cap over in his hands.

'What if I could get your sentence commuted?' he asked. 'To enrollment in Project Unity.'

'And wind up like Beck? Never.'

Chiron sighed. 'If you won't listen to me, what about him? Let me send Beck to your cell, to talk. Do that for me at least, Zare.'

'All right,' Zare said. 'It won't do any good, but all right.'

* * *

Zare had just given up on a tasteless portion of cold nerf stew when the guards let Beck into his cell. When his former friend and teammate sat and looked at him, Zare suppressed a slight shiver. It was like Beck was looking through Zare, his eyes seeing something visible only to him.

'We match now,' Beck said, pointing at Zare's orange jumpsuit and smiling. 'You should listen to Lieutenant Chiron, you know. He wants to help you. Project Unity helped me.'

'Helped you how? By brainwashing you into some kind of droid? By feeding you drugs?'

'It's not like that at all, Zare,' Beck said. 'The medications calm you and give you clarity so you can consider other points of view. That's all. They're helpful. I had to stop taking them so they could question me for your tribunal, and I miss them. But look at me – I'm no different. I just see things differently now.'

Zare looked at him in horror, then shook his head.

'Do you remember the day we rode out to the camp in the Westhills?' Zare asked. 'The one the displaced people had set up near your family's orchards? The orchards the Empire ruined?'

'I remember,' Beck said. 'Our orchards were beautiful.'

'The farmers were waiting for an Imperial

representative to come talk to them. But when he did, he told them to disperse – that their assembly was illegal. And then the stormtroopers started to beat people. And to stun them. And finally they shot to kill. Do you remember that, Beck?'

'Yes,' Beck said with eerie calm. 'We took my family's jumpspeeders – the unregistered ones that couldn't be tracked. I remember. The difference is now I understand what I didn't then. Those people didn't know it, but they were being used by the Empire's enemies – greedy, secretive organisations that want to return the galaxy to corruption and disorder. It's hard, but the Empire has to deny those enemies the use of their tools – by whatever means necessary. If the contagion of separatism ever gets loose again it will infect the entire galaxy, not just one world.'

'Those were Imperial citizens back on Lothal, Beck! People you knew! The Empire murdered them!'

'The Empire did what it had to do to protect everyone. If you want to stop things like that, join Project Unity. Fight the real enemies – the people in the shadows who tricked those farmers into endangering themselves. The ones pulling the strings.'

'This is pointless,' Zare said in disgust. 'Get out.'

'I'm sorry you don't want to be helped,' Beck said. He spoke into his comlink and got to his feet. A minute later the door opened. It was Chiron again, flanked by two stormtroopers. Beck gave Zare a last smile and exited, leaving Chiron standing uncertainly in the doorway.

'Don't start – I'd rather die than become a Project Unity drone,' Zare said.

Chiron sighed.

'Then there's nothing left to do but ask what you want for your last meal in the morning,' he said. 'And who you'd like to bring it.'

'How about a properly prepared nerf steak?' Zare asked. 'Brought by a pirate captain with a fast ship for hire.'

Chiron smiled thinly. 'I'm afraid not. I thought I'd bring the meal, if that's all right with you.'

Zare turned away from his former mentor's gaze. He smelled the salt air. It made him think about Merei and how she'd talked of poetry, of memory.

He looked back at Chiron.

'Send Beck again,' he said. 'He's the only one here who I knew before everything went wrong.'

'All right. And your last meal? You can have anything you want – except for that pirate ship.'

'I won't need anything that fancy,' Zare said, and told Chiron what he wanted.

# CHAPTER 20

**They had** to wake Zare in the morning. He sat up on his bunk with a start, staring into the unfriendly face of an Imperial officer. The man withdrew with a scowl, and Beck entered Zare's cell, followed by a droid with a covered tray. The droid placed the tray on Zare's bunk and departed, leaving the two of them alone.

'Do you remember Lothal, Beck?' Zare asked.

His former friend shook his head. 'Not this again. I know what you're going to try to do, Zare. It didn't work when we talked last night, and it won't work now. I remember everything about Lothal – I haven't forgotten anything.'

'I think you have,' Zare said, picking up the tray. He stood in front of Beck and lifted the cover, praying that his request had been honoured.

The tray was empty except for two jogan fruits, their

skins deep purple, their stems crowned with sprigs of blossoms. Zare handed one to Beck.

'Smell that,' he said. 'It will remind you of home.'

Beck blinked at Zare for a moment, then raised the fruit to his nose. He sniffed it and his eyes closed. Zare sat down on his bunk, trying to get his breath as Beck inhaled the fragrance of the blossoms.

Beck's hand opened, and the fruit hit the floor of the cell.

'They . . . they destroyed everything,' Beck said, and tears began to run down his face.

'Yes, they did,' Zare said.

'And when people wanted it to stop they killed them.'

Zare nodded.

'They . . . they did things to me, Zare.'

'I know. It's not your fault. They've done things to a lot of people.'

Beck looked down at his hands. 'Your sister?' he asked.

Zare nodded. 'Dhara's alive – somewhere in this tower.'

Beck reached down to the fallen jogan and pulled the sprig of blossoms from its stalk. He smelled it again, then wiped at his wet cheeks.

'Are you all right?' Zare asked.

'I don't know,' Beck said. 'It's hard to think straight. But I think so.'

He closed his eyes, took a deep breath, then opened them again. He looked at Zare, eyes clearer.

'Let's go get your sister,' he said.

Zare smiled. 'Do you know the layout of the tower?'

'No,' Beck said with a frown. 'We're above where Project Unity meets – we share the ceremonial room with the Academy cadets. I've never been up here.'

'Well, that's unfortunate,' Zare said. 'I'm thinking we find my sister and fight our way to the roof. That's where ships carrying important people land, so maybe the commandant has a transport up there.'

'Right. But how do we get past the two stormtroopers outside?'

'I was thinking a handoff and a centre-striker sneak. You remember the play?'

'I do. You ready?'

'Not really.'

'Me neither.'

'Let's do this then,' Zare said.

Beck pulled out his comlink. 'The prisoner's not quite done with breakfast, but I'm ready to come out,' he said, then lowered his shoulders, staring at the door as if it were the centre line on a grav-ball grid. Zare got behind him, ready to spring.

The door slid aside and Beck rammed himself into the stormtrooper's midsection. Zare was right behind him, hands outstretched to take the blaster Beck had wrested from the trooper's hands. He fired at the other guard, who fell with a clatter of armour, then turned and shot the stormtrooper struggling with Beck.

'Come on – hurry,' Zare said, rushing down the short corridor past the other cells. Beck picked up the other trooper's E-11 and followed. He nodded at Zare, who thumbed open the door and blasted the startled guards in the detention block's control room.

'Shoot out the cameras while I try to find Dhara,' he told Beck, scanning the room. Three doors led to cell bays. On the other side of the room was an elevator and a smaller door of wood. And on the wall behind Zare and Beck was a door to another, smaller elevator.

Zare shoved an officer's body aside and examined the computer console, then began typing rapidly, trying to navigate the unfamiliar displays.

'Come on, Sis, where are you?' he muttered.

Engines roared overhead, rising in pitch and then cutting off. A ship had landed on the top of the tower. Alarms began to blare, and a moment later Zare's monitor went blank.

'We're about to be surrounded,' Beck said. 'Did you find her?'

'No – they just shut me out of the system.'

The elevator indicator chimed.

'Get down!' Beck said as the doors opened and stormtroopers advanced into the control room. Zare shot the leader in the chest, knocking him backward into his two comrades as the two boys filled the elevator with laser fire. The Imperials lay motionless, but now footsteps clattered on the stairs.

'Hit them fast and hard,' Zare said, rushing to take cover behind another console so he and Beck could fire on the door from two angles.

Laser blasts sounded above them and they looked at each other in surprise. Then the wooden door flew open and Zare fired wildly at the shapes on the other side. Something bright intercepted the blasts, sending them ricocheting around the control room.

'Zare!' someone with a familiar voice yelled. Zare frantically signalled Beck to stop shooting.

It couldn't be.

'Merei?' he asked in disbelief.

Merei pushed past a towering alien, a slim girl in Mandalorian armour, and Dev Morgan – who was holding a glowing energy blade. Merei fell into Zare's arms as everybody began talking at once. Zare ignored the tumult and held her against him for a long moment.

Then he stepped back and stared at her, barely able to believe she was real.

'What are you . . . how did you . . .' he stammered.

Merei smiled. 'I came to rescue you, of course – though it looks like you've been rescuing yourselves. You know Dev Morgan, and these are his friends, the Spectres. And your mum and dad are safe on Garel.'

She turned and hugged Beck as Dev offered Zare the cocky grin Zare had once found so infuriating.

'Don't tell me you missed me, Zare,' he said.

'Better believe it, cadet,' Zare said, then turned back to Merei. 'I'm glad to see you, but the Imperials have locked down the network and we don't even know the layout of the tower.'

'It's a good thing we're here, then, because Mum and I know it,' Merei said, nodding at a petite, dark-eyed woman behind her.

'Now that we're all caught up, time for business,' said the armoured girl. 'Spectre-4 and I will take Jessa down to the main computer node and lock the Imperials out of the tower and the elevators. Merei, slice into the network up here and get Zare's sister. Spectre-6, you hold the roof so we can get out of here. Then, if we get back to Garel quick enough, *maybe* Spectre-2 will forgive us for stealing her ship.'

'We ain't stealin' it, exactly,' the big alien objected with a sheepish look. 'More like borrowin' it for a bit.'

'You can explain it to her, then,' the Mandalorian girl said, taking a shiny silver ball off her belt. She activated the thermal detonator, then tossed it down the stairwell. A moment later a muffled thump shook the tower.

'That ought to discourage any welcoming committees down below,' she said with satisfaction. She tossed Merei another detonator. 'And here's a special gift for you to give that certain Imperial someone.'

'Are those gonna make a pretty explosion?' the alien asked with a grin.

'Didn't have time for anything fancy,' said the Mandalorian girl, sounding disappointed. 'But they'll make a big mess.'

'I s'pose that's good enough,' the hulking alien said.

Jessa nodded to Merei and followed the Spectres down the stairs. A pale Merei gingerly handed the detonator to Beck and plugged her datapad into the dormant computer console.

'I already know Dhara's in cell seventeen, but it'll take me a minute to get around the lockdown coding so we can get to her,' she said. 'Watch that door to our rear – it's an auxiliary lift restricted to high-ranking personnel.'

'I've got it,' Zare said. 'Beck, cover the main elevator.'

'Will do. You know what I was just thinking about? Grav-ball.'

'Grav-ball?' Merei asked, typing frantically.

'Yep. How many points are we losing by, and how much time is left on the clock?'

'Who says we're losing?' Zare asked.

'We're in a tower surrounded by stormtroopers and we're locked out of the computer system. I wouldn't call that winning.'

'It's the final score that matters – and we're not there yet. Speaking of which, how are we doing, Merei?'

'Almost there,' Merei said, and then her comlink buzzed.

'It's Spectre-5,' said the Mandalorian girl. 'We've locked down the tower, but watch yourselves – there are bucketheads between you and us.'

'Acknowledged,' Merei said. Then her voice rose: 'Got it!'

The detention-block door slid aside.

'Go get Dhara, Zare,' Merei said. 'If I can get that auxiliary elevator running we can go straight to the roof.'

Zare hurried down the corridor. Cell seventeen was

identical to the others – a featureless black slab of a door. He hesitated and thumbed it open.

Dhara Leonis was lying on the bunk in the dimly lit cell, huddled in a ball. Her eyes flew open and her hands jerked up, clenched in fists.

'Dhara – it's me,' he said. 'It's Zare.'

His sister stared at him uncomprehendingly. Then she shrank back into the corner of the cell, one eye peering at him above her shoulder.

'Come on, Sis,' he said gently. 'We have to go.'

'Zare?' she asked, her voice a croak. Then her eyes went wild and her feet scrabbled at the metal bunk, trying to propel herself away from him.

'No,' she moaned. 'No, no, no. This isn't real. You're a dream – but this one isn't true. It's one of his tricks . . .'

'I *am* real,' Zare said. 'And the person who did this to you is dead. He can't hurt you anymore – you or anyone else. Now you need to come with me.'

'Dead?' Dhara asked, looking doubtfully at her brother's outstretched hand.

'He's dead – I promise,' Zare said, edging closer to the frightened girl. 'Don't be scared – just take my hand. Mum and Dad are waiting for us.'

Still staring at Zare, Dhara slowly stretched out her hand. He took it gently. His sister was trembling violently.

'That's it. Good. Now come on, Sis.'

Dhara rose shakily to her feet, staring at her hand in Zare's. He put his arm around her.

'Zare,' she said. 'It really is you.'

Blaster fire erupted nearby. Keeping one arm around his sister, Zare peeked out of the cell – only to find Merei and Beck retreating down the corridor from the control room.

'Stormtroopers,' Beck said. 'We had to fall back.'

'It's all right, Sis,' Zare said, though he very much doubted that was true. Dhara said nothing but clung to him, her eyes wide and staring.

Merei brought her comlink up to her mouth. 'Spectres, we're cut off in the cell bay!'

'Unfortunately, so are we,' the Mandalorian girl said.

'And there are TIEs inbound,' Dev said grimly.

# CHAPTER 21

**A laser** blast struck above Zare's head and he stepped in front of his cowering sister, squeezing off a barrage of shots at the troopers in the control room.

'We're not going to last five minutes if we stay here,' he said.

'Agreed – too bad we can't leave,' Merei said, flattening herself against the wall.

'We can and we will,' Beck said. 'Tell your mum and the Spectres to start up the stairs. I'll take care of the troopers – one way or another.'

He hefted the detonator Spectre-5 had given Merei, finger on the trigger.

'Beck, no – you'll never make it,' Zare said.

'It's a fullback carry. How many games did we win with it?'

'The other team didn't have blasters,' Merei said. 'Beck, you can't!'

‘Somebody has to, before more Imperials come,’ Beck said. ‘Or you’ll all die here – you and your friends.’

‘Beck, we’ll think of another way,’ Zare pleaded.

‘There isn’t one. Now listen to me. Lothal needs you. You’re the ones I’d been hoping for – the ones who will spark the fire that turns the Empire to ash. And besides, you never know – I might get lucky.’

Before Zare and Merei could object, Beck raised his blaster and charged into the control room, screaming at the top of his lungs. Merei followed, her own pistol spitting fire, and Zare pulled at Dhara’s hand.

Then a thunderclap of sound and a blast of air knocked them backward.

Zare got to his feet, half-dragging his sister behind him. His ears hurt. The control room was silent and filled with smoke. A huge hole had been blown in the elevator doors, and a pile of stone chunks and jagged metal blocked the doorway to the stairs. Merei was staring at the debris, one hand over her mouth.

Zare went and stood beside her. He saw Beck’s arm extending from beneath the fallen stone. The sprig of jogan blossoms was in his fingers.

Zare heard faint sounds from the blocked doorway to the stairs. Then Merei’s comlink chimed.

‘We’re right next to you, but we can’t get through,’ said the big Lasat.

Merei rushed to the computer console and set her pistol down beside it. The screen was shattered.

'Maybe we could climb up the main elevator shaft,' she said. 'There has to be an emergency ladder, right?'

Zare tried to imagine leading his sister up such a ladder, if it even existed. Dhara staggered, one hand going to her mouth, and Merei rushed to her side.

Then the auxiliary elevator dinged. The door opened and Chiron stepped into the control room, followed by four stormtroopers. All had their blasters raised.

'It's over, Zare,' Chiron said.

Merei looked helplessly at her pistol, where she'd left it on the computer console. Zare, blaster raised, stepped between the Imperials and the two girls, trying to give them whatever slight cover his body could offer.

'I'm warning you,' he told Chiron. 'Not one more step.'

'You're outnumbered, Zare. Please don't make me do this.'

'If you do we'll both die,' Zare said. 'Do you know who this is? This is my sister, Dhara. Look at what the Empire did to her. Think about what it's done to the people of Lothal. And so many other planets.'

'Zare, drop your weapon. Do it for your sister's sake. I promise you she won't be harmed.'

'That won't save her!' Zare shouted, staring down

the barrel of his gun at Chiron. 'It won't save anybody! The Empire you believe in only exists in your head! You have to see that!'

Chiron looked at Zare and his face twisted in misery. But then he shook his head.

'Everything that's happened will be investigated, and if there's been wrongdoing it will be punished,' he said. 'But I will do my duty.'

Dhara pushed at Merei, the movement uncertain. She took one shuffling step forward, hands raised as if in prayer.

'No,' she said, the word barely audible. Chiron's eyes turned to the stricken young woman.

And then Dhara's arms snapped out at her sides and she shrieked in rage and pain. For a split second Merei thought she saw the young woman's eyes burning like fire. Merei ducked as chunks of rock and metal flew past them, as if flung by some invisible and immensely strong hand. The debris pummelled Chiron and the stormtroopers, and Merei heard armour crack. The Imperials fell and lay still on the deck.

Dhara lowered her arms and her shoulders slumped. The fusillade of stone and metal had ended as quickly as it had begun. Dhara stared down at her hands, blinking in confusion, then clung to her brother.

'Quick! Into the elevator!' Merei said.

Zare knelt beside Chiron. The officer's eyes were open and lifeless, his head at an unnatural angle. Zare leaned forward and closed Chiron's eyes, then led Dhara into the elevator. Merei was on her comlink, telling the Spectres to get to the roof.

'What . . . what was that?' Merei asked Zare when the doors closed. He didn't have to ask her what she meant.

'I don't know,' he said. 'But don't tell anybody. I mean it, Merei.'

She nodded and the doors opened. Rain lashed their faces. Dev stood in front of a deadly-looking modified freighter's ramp. He saw them and motioned for them to hurry. The Lasat and the armoured girl were running across the roof from the other direction, followed by Merei's mother.

When the TIE fighters arrived above the tower, the freighter was just a speck in the distance, hurtling away over the dark sea.

# CHAPTER 22

**Once they** were safely in hyperspace, Zare and Merei led Dhara to a bunk aboard the ship. She lay down without speaking, her eyes fixed on the bunk above her.

'Give us a minute?' Zare asked Merei, smiling apologetically.

'Of course,' she said, squeezing his hand.

When Merei was gone, Zare gently placed his hand on Dhara's forehead.

'Hey, Sis,' he said quietly, smiling. 'It's all right. We're safe.'

Dhara's eyes fluttered, then turned his way.

'I knew you would come,' she said. 'I dreamed it.'

'And you were right,' Zare said, feeling his eyes well up.

'I saw it,' Dhara said. 'I saw the way it happened. I saw you, and that girl.'

'Merei,' Zare said.

'And the boy beneath the rocks,' Dhara said. 'I dreamed so many things, Zare. He'd force me to tell him about them. He was so angry when I couldn't remember.'

'Shhh,' Zare said. 'He's gone.'

Dhara looked at him, her mouth moving silently. Then she shook her head.

'There were stormtroopers there,' she said. 'I remember that. And a man. He knew you. But . . . I can't remember what happened next.'

'That's all right,' Zare said. 'It's over now. Get some rest.'

Dhara nodded slowly, then reached up to touch Zare's cheek.

'It really is you, Zare,' she murmured. 'I'm so tired, but I don't want to sleep. I'm afraid I'll wake up and this will all have been another dream.'

'It isn't,' Zare said. 'I'm real, and you're safe. Now go to sleep. When you wake up I'll be here and Mum and Dad will be waiting.'

Dhara looked at him and smiled tentatively.

'You promise?'

'I promise.'

Dhara nodded and closed her eyes. Zare waited

until her chest began to rise and fall evenly, then got to his feet and crept out of the cabin.

He found Dev waiting outside the cabin door.

'Is your sister all right?' he asked.

'I think so,' Zare said. 'She's been through a lot. Thank you, Dev.'

Dev looked embarrassed.

'I should have told you before,' he said. 'My name's not Dev.'

Zare smiled.

'So what is it really?'

'Ezra. Ezra Bridger. '

'Then thank you, Ezra. After all this time, it's nice to be truly introduced.'

'Better late than never, right? When we get to Garel I'll introduce you to the rest of my friends.'

As the *Ghost* neared Garel, Merei took Zare a mug of tea and squeezed in beside him on the acceleration couch in the freighter's hold. Despite the crowded conditions aboard the Spectres' ship, they were alone: Dhara was still asleep; Ezra was in the cockpit with Zeb; and Jessa and Sabine were comparing slicing strategies.

Zare put his arm around Merei and she rested her head on his shoulder.

'I've missed you,' she said.

'Me too,' Zare said. 'I can't tell you how much. When I saw you come through that door – well, I swore if we made it out alive I'd never let you go again.'

Merei smiled and kissed him. 'That sounds good to me.'

They sat in silence for a few minutes, simply enjoying being next to each other.

'What happens now, though?' Zare asked.

Merei sighed. 'My father's working on new identities for both our families. And we'll need a new world to call home, I suppose. It's a big galaxy – we can find something away from all this.'

'I suppose.'

Merei turned to look at Zare. 'That didn't sound very convincing.'

'I've seen how powerful the Empire is – and how powerful it will become if it isn't stopped. The commandant at the Academy had a vision of an Empire that will rule the galaxy forever.'

Merei nodded. 'And you want to keep fighting.'

'That's the last thing I want,' Zare said with a sigh. 'But what choice do we have?'

'That's how Ezra and his friends see it, too,' Merei said. 'We could help them.'

'I get the feeling they're part of a larger struggle, but I keep thinking about Lothal – and about Beck. He gave his life for us, and it wasn't so we could run and hide. It was so we could carry on the fight.'

Merei was quiet for a moment. Then she smiled and shook her head.

'Every time I think I've escaped trouble I find myself running right back into it,' she said. 'But since you mention it, I downloaded thousands of classified documents from the Imperial network on Lothal. There's economic plans and industrial-production reports, but also a lot of military intel you'd understand a lot better than I can. So maybe there's something in there that will prove useful to us.'

'I bet you're right,' Zare said with a smile.

The *Ghost* settled with the tiniest of bumps on a landing platform overlooking the towers of Garel City.

'Last stop – everybody off,' said Zeb, indicating the ramp with a flourish of one big purple hand. 'Not that it ain't been fun, you understand.'

'Maybe we'll do it again sometime,' Merei said, standing on her tiptoes to give the big Lasat a kiss on the cheek, above his hairy jawline.

'Are you blushing, Zeb?' Zare heard Ezra ask as Merei and Jessa descended the gangplank. He grinned as the argument escalated behind him and Dhara.

'Mum and Dad are here,' he said, holding his sister's hand. 'Are you ready?'

Dhara nodded and squeezed his fingers. 'Ready,' she said in a small voice.

Zare and Dhara walked down the ramp, blinking as they emerged from the *Ghost*'s dim interior. Zare realised he'd braced himself for rain, but Garel was bathed in brilliant sunshine.

Zare smiled at the sight of Gandr Spanjaf at the bottom of the ramp, hugging Merei and Jessa. Then he saw his own parents. Zare glanced at Dhara, alert for any sign of fear, but his sister was looking at Leo and Tepha. She smiled tentatively, then more confidently. And then she let go of Zare's hand, raised her arms, and vanished into their mother's embrace.

Tepha rocked her daughter back and forth, cheeks wet with tears, as Leo pulled Zare into his arms and thumped his son on the back. Leo and Tepha got tangled up trying to hug both of their children at once, then simply gathered in everyone they could reach.

'Mum, Dad,' Dhara said from the middle of their warm, happy knot. 'Don't let go. Don't let go.'

And, for a very long time, no one did.

# ABOUT THE AUTHOR

**Jason Fry** is the author of the Jupiter Pirates young adult space-fantasy series and has written or cowritten some two dozen novels, short stories, and other works set in the galaxy far, far away, including *The Essential Atlas* and *The Clone Wars Episode Guide.* He lives in Brooklyn, New York, with his wife, son, and about a metric ton of *Star Wars* stuff.